P9-CWE-088

FICTION

# STORY OF MY LIFE

BY THE SAME AUTHOR

*Bright Lights, Big City*
*Ransom*

A NOVEL BY

JAY McINERNEY

THE ATLANTIC MONTHLY PRESS
NEW YORK

*The author wishes to thank the Corporation of Yaddo, where this book was written.*



All resemblance to actual persons, living or dead, is purely coincidental.

*Story of My Life* is based on a story that appeared in *Esquire.*

An excerpt from the novel was published in the premiere issue of *Smart* magazine.



*Published simultaneously in Canada by McClelland & Stewart, Toronto*
*Printed in the United States of America*

Library of Congress Cataloging-in-Publication data
McInerney, Jay.
Story of my life : a novel / by Jay McInerney. — 1st ed.
ISBN 0-87113-238-9
I. Title.
PS3563.C3694S76 1988 813'.54—dc19 88-10323

Design by Laura Hough

The Atlantic Monthly Press
19 Union Square West
New York, NY 10003

FIRST PRINTING

For Gary

# CONTENTS

*The age of Cronos was in general characterized as the age of anarchy, the time before the institution of property, the establishment of cities, or the framing of laws. We may fairly infer that it was not gods, but humans, who first became dissatisfied with the blessings of anarchy.*

*—Philip Velacott, introduction to The Oresteian Trilogy*

# 1 GETTING IN TOUCH WITH YOUR CHILD

I'm like, I don't believe this shit.

I'm totally pissed at my old man who's somewhere in the Virgin Islands, I don't know where. The check wasn't in the mailbox today which means I can't go to school Monday morning. I'm on the monthly payment program because Dad says wanting to be an actress is some flaky whim and I never stick to anything—this from a guy who's been married five times—and this way if I drop out in the middle of the semester he won't get burned for the full tuition. Meanwhile he buys his new bimbo Tanya who's a year younger than me a 450 SL convertible—always gone for the young ones, haven't we, Dad?—plus her own condo so she can have some privacy to do her writing. Like she can even *read.* He actually believes her when she says she's writing a novel but when I want to spend eight hours a day busting ass at Lee Strasberg it's like, *another one of Alison's crazy ideas.* Story of my life. My old man is fifty-two going on twelve. And then there's Skip Pendleton, which is another reason I'm pissed.

So I'm on the phone screaming at my father's secretary when there's a call on my other line. I go hello and this guy goes, hi, I'm whatever-his-name-is, I'm a friend of Skip's and I say yeah? and he says, I thought maybe we could go out sometime.

And I say, what am I, dial-a-date?

Skip Pendleton's this jerk I was in lust with once for about three minutes. He hasn't called me in like three weeks which is fine, okay, I can deal with that, but suddenly I'm like a baseball card he trades with his friends? Give me a break. So I go to this guy, what makes you think I'd want to go out with you, I don't even know you? and he says, Skip told me about you. Right. So I'm like, what did he tell you? and the guy goes—Skip said you were hot. I say, great, I'm totally honored that the great Skip Pendleton thinks I'm hot. I'm just a jalapeño pepper waiting for some strange burrito, honey. I mean, *really.*

And this guy says to me, we were sitting around at Skip's place about five in the morning the other night wired out of our minds and I say—this is the guy talking—I wish we had some women and Skip is like, I could always call Alison, she'd be over like a shot.

He said that? I say. I can hear his voice exactly, it's not like I'm totally amazed, but still I can't believe even *he* would be such a pig and suddenly I feel like a cheap slut and I want to scream at this asshole but instead I say, where are you? He's on West Eighty-ninth, it figures, so I give him an address on Avenue C, a rathole where a friend of mine lived last year until her place was broken into for the seventeenth time and which is about as far away from the Upper West Side as you can get without crossing water, so I tell him to meet me there in an hour and at least I have the satisfaction of thinking of him spending about twenty bucks for a cab and then hanging around the doorway of this tenement and maybe getting beat up by some drug dealers. But the one I'm really pissed at is Skip Pendleton. Nothing my father does surprises me anymore. I'm twenty going on gray.

Skip is thirty-one and he's so smart and so educated—just ask him, he'll tell you. A legend in his own mind. Did I forget to mention he's *so* mature? Unlike me. He was always telling me I don't know anything. I'll tell you one thing I don't know—I don't know what I saw in him. He seemed older and sophisticated and we had great sex, so why not? I met him in a club, naturally. I never thought he was very good-looking, but you could tell *he* thought he was. He believed it so much he could actually sell other people on the idea. He has that confidence everybody wants a piece of. This blond hair that looks like he has it trimmed about three times a day. Nice clothes, shirts custom-made on Jermyn Street, which he might just casually tell you some night in case you didn't know is in London, England. (That's in Europe, which is across the Atlantic Ocean—oh, really Skip, is that where it is? Wow!) Went to the right schools. And he's rich, of course, owns his own company. Commodities trader. Story of Skip's life, trading commodities.

So basically, he has it all. Should be a Dewar's Profile, I'm like amazed they haven't asked him yet. But when the sun hit him in the morning he was a shivering wreck.

From the first night, bending over the silver picture frame in his apartment with a rolled fifty up his nose, all he can talk about is his ex, and how if he could only get her back he'd give up all of this forever—coke, staying out partying all night, young bimbos like me. And I'm thinking, poor guy just lost his main squeeze, feeling real sympathetic and so like I go, when did this happen, Skip? and it turns out it was ten years ago! He lived with this chick for four years at Harvard and then after they come to New York together she dumps him. And I'm like, give me a break, Skip. Give yourself a break. This is ten years after. This is nineteen eighty-whatever.

Skip's so smart, right? My parents never gave a shit whether I went to school or not, they were off chasing lovers and bottles, leaving us kids with the cars and the credit cards, and I never did get much of an education. Is that my fault? I mean, if someone told you back then that you could either go to school or not, what do you think you would have done? Pass the trigonometry, please. Right. So I'm not as educated as the great Skip Pendleton, but let me tell you—I know that when you're hitting on someone you don't spend the whole night whining about your ex, especially after like a decade. And you don't need a Ph.D. in psychology to figure out why Skip can't go out with anybody his own age. He keeps trying to find Diana, the beautiful, perfect Diana who was twenty-one when she said sayonara. And he wants us, the young stuff, because we're like Diana was in the good old days. And he hates us because we're not Diana. And he thinks it will make him feel better if he fucks us over and makes us hurt the way he was hurt, because that's what it's all about if you ask me—we're all sitting around here on earth working through our hurts, trying to pass them along to other people and make things even. Chain of pain.

Old Skip kept telling me how dumb I was. You wish, Jack. Funny thing is, dumb is his type. He doesn't want to go out with anybody who might see through him, so he picks up girls like me. Girls he thinks will believe everything he says and fuck him the first night and not be real surprised when he never calls again.

If you're so smart, Skip, how come you don't know these things? If you're so mature, what were you doing with me?

Men. I've never met any. They're all boys. I wish I didn't want them so much. I've had a few dreams about making it with girls, but it's kind of like—sure, I'd love to visit Norway sometime. My roommate Jeannie and I sleep in the same bed and it's great. We've got a one-bedroom and this way the living room is free for partying and whatever. I hate being alone, but when I wake up in some guy's bed with dry come on the sheets and he's snoring like a garbage truck, I go—let me out of here. I slip out and crawl around the floor groping for my clothes, trying to untangle his blue jeans from mine, my bra from his Jockeys—Skip wears boxers, of course—without making any noise, out the door and home to where Jeannie has been warming the bed all night. Jumping in between the sheets and she wakes up and goes, I want details, Alison—length and width.

I love Jeannie. She cracks me up. She's an assistant editor at a fashion magazine but what she really wants to do is get married. It might work for her but I don't believe in it. My parents have seven marriages between them and any time I've been with a guy for more than a few weeks I find myself looking out the window during sex.

I call up my friend Didi to see if she can lend me the money. Didi's father's rich and he gives her this huge allowance, but she spends it all on blow. She used to buy clothes but now she wears the same outfit for four or five days in a row and it's pretty gross, let me tell you. Sometimes we have to send the health department over to her apartment to open the windows and burn the sheets.

I get Didi's machine, which means she's not home. If she's home she unplugs the phone and if she's not home she turns on the answering machine. Either way it's pretty impossible to get hold of her. She sleeps from about noon till like 9:00 P.M. or so. If Didi made a list of her favorite things I guess cocaine would be at the top and sunlight wouldn't even make the cut.

My friends and I spend half our lives leaving messages for each other. Luckily I know Didi's message access code so I dial again and listen to her messages to see if I can figure out from the messages where she is. Okay, maybe I'm just nosy.

The first message is from Wick and from his voice I can tell that he's doing Didi, which really blows me away, since Wick is Jeannie's old boyfriend. Except that Didi is less interested in sex than anybody I know so I'm not really sure. Maybe Wick is just starting to make his move. A message from her mom—call me, sweetie, I'm in Aspen. Then Emile, saying he wants his three hundred and fifty dollars or else. Which is when I go—what am I, crazy? I'm never going to get a cent out of Didi. If I even try she'll talk me into getting wired with her and I'm trying to stay away from that. I'm about to hang up when I get a call on the other line. It's my school telling me that my tuition hasn't arrived and that I can't come back to class until it does. Like, what do you think I've been frantic about for the last twenty-four hours? It's Saturday afternoon. Jeannie will be home soon and then it's all over.

By this time I'm getting pretty bitter. You could say I am not a happy unit. Acting is the first thing I've ever really wanted to do. Except for riding. When I was a kid I spent most of my time on horseback. I went around the country, showing my horses and jumping, until Dangerous Dan dropped dead. I loved Dan more than just about any living thing since and that was it for me and horses. That's what happens, basically, when you love something. It's like, you can't get rid of the shit you don't like, I have this rotten crinoline dress that's been following me from apartment to apartment for years, but every time I find something I really love one of my sisters or girlfriends disappears with it the next day. Actually, we all trade clothes, hardly anybody I know would think of leaving the house without wearing something borrowed or stolen, if it was just clothes I'd be like, no problem, but that's another story.

So anyway, after horses I got into drugs. But acting, I don't know, I just love it, getting up there and turning myself inside out. Being somebody else for a change. It's like being a child again, playing at something, making believe, laughing and crying all over the place, ever since I can remember people have been trying to get me to stifle my emotions but forget it—I'm an emotional kind of girl. My drama teacher has this great thing he always says—get in touch with your child, which is supposed to be the raw, uncensored part of yourself. Acting is about being true to your feelings, which is great since real life seems to be about being a liar and a hypocrite.

Acting is the first thing that's made me get up in the morning. The first year I was in New York I didn't do anything but guys and blow. Staying out all night at the Surf Club and Zulu, waking up at five in the afternoon with plugged sinuses and sticky hair. Some kind of white stuff in every opening. Story of my life. My friends are still pretty much that way which is why I'm so desperate to get this check because if I don't then there's no reason to wake up early Monday morning and Jeannie will get home and somebody will call up and the next thing I know it'll be three days from now with no sleep in between, brain in orbit, nose in traction. I call my father's secretary again and she says she's still trying to reach him.

I decide to do some of my homework before Jeannie gets home—my sense-memory exercise. Don't ask me why, since I won't be able to go to school. But it chills me out. I sit down in the folding chair and relax, empty my mind of all the crap. Then I begin to imagine an orange. I try to see it in front of me. I take it in my hand. A big old round one veined with rust, like the ones you get down in Florida straight from the tree. (Those Clearasil spotless ones you buy in the Safeway are dusted with cyanide or some such shit so you can imagine how good they are for you.) So I start to peel it real slow, smelling the little geysers of spray that break from the squeezed peel, feeling the juice stinging around the edges of my fingernails where I've bitten them. . . .

So of course the phone rings. A guy's voice, Barry something, says, may I please speak to Alison Poole?

And I'm like, you're doing it.

I'm a friend of Skip's, he says.

I go, if this is some kind of joke I'm like really not amused.

Hey, no joke, he goes. I'm just, you know, Skip told me you guys weren't going out anymore and I saw you once at Indochine and I thought maybe we could do dinner sometime.

I'm like, I don't believe this. What am I?—the York Avenue Escort Service?

I go, did Skip also tell you about the disease he gave me? That shrinks this Barry's equipment pretty quick. Suddenly he's got a call on his other line. Sure you do.

It's true—that was Skip's little going-away present. Morning after the last night I slept with him I was really sore and itchy and then I get this weird rash so I finally go to the doctor who gives me this big lecture on AIDS—yada yada yada—then says the rash is a sexually transmitted thing that won't kill me but I have to take these antibiotics for two weeks and not sleep with anybody in the meantime. I go, two weeks, who do you think I am, the Virgin Mary? and she goes, as your doctor I think I know your habits well enough to know what a sacrifice this will be for you, Alison. Then she gives me the usual about why don't I make them wear condoms and I'm like, for the same reason I don't fuck with my clothes on, you can't beat flesh on flesh. I want contact, right? Just give me direct contact and you can keep true love.

Anyway I never did tell Skip, I don't know why, I guess I just didn't want to talk to him, the son of a bitch.

So I'm smoking a cigarette, thumbing through my *Actors' Scenebook,* sort of looking for a monologue, I've got to get one for next week but I haven't found anything I like, I start browsing around the other sections, Monologues for Men, Scenes for Two Women—no thanks—Scenes for One Man and One Woman. Which is about the worst scene there is.

The phone rings again and it's Didi. Unbelievable! Live—in person, practically. And it's daylight outside.

I just went to my nose doctor, she goes. He was horrified. Told me that if I had to keep doing blow I should start shooting up, then the damage would be some other doctor's responsibility.

What's with you and Wick? I say.

I don't know, she goes, I went home with him a couple of weeks ago. I woke up in his bed. I'm not even sure we did anything. But he's definitely in lust with me. Meanwhile, my period's late. So maybe we did.

Didi has another call. While she takes it, I'm thinking. The wheels are turning—wheels within wheels. Didi comes back on and tells me it's her mom, who's having a major breakdown, she'll call me back. I tell her no problem. She's already been a big help.

I get Skip at his office. He doesn't sound too thrilled to hear from me. He says he's in a meeting, can he call me back?

I say no, I have to talk now.

What's up? he says.

I go, I'm pregnant.

Total silence.

Before he can ask I tell him I haven't slept with anybody else in six weeks. Which is totally true, almost. Close off that little escape hatch in his mind. Wham, bam, thank you ma'am.

He goes, you're sure? He sounds like he's just swallowed a bunch of sand.

I'm sure, I say.

He's like, what do you want to do?

The thing about Skip is that even though he's an asshole, he's also a gentleman. Actually a lot of the assholes I know are gentlemen. Or vice versa. Dickheads with a family crest and a prep-school code of honor.

When I say I need money he asks how much.

A thousand, I say. I can't believe I ask him for that much, I was thinking five hundred just a minute ago, but hearing his voice pisses me off.

He asks if I want him to go with me and I say no, definitely not. Then he tries to do this number about making out the check directly to the clinic and I say, Skip, don't give me that shit. I need five hundred in cash to make the appointment, I tell him, and I don't want to wait six business days for the stupid check to clear, okay? Acting my ass off. My teacher would be proud.

Two hours later a messenger arrives with the money. Cash. I give him a ten-dollar tip.

Saturday night Jeannie and Didi go out. Didi comes over, wearing this same horrible surfer shirt she's had on all week and her blond rastafarian hair. Really gross. But she's still incredibly beautiful, even after four days without sleep, and guys make total asses of themselves trying to pick her up. Her mother was this really big model in the fifties, Swedish. Didi was supposed to be the Revlon Girl or something but she couldn't be bothered to wake up for the shoot.

Jeannie's wearing my black cashmere sweater, a couple yards of pearls, jeans and Maude Frizon pumps.

How do I look? she goes, checking herself out in the mirror.

Terrific, I say. You'll be lucky if you make it through cocktails without getting raped.

Can't rape the willing, Jeannie says, which is what we always say.

They try to get me to come along, but I'm doing my scene for class Monday morning. They can't believe it. They say it won't last. I go, this is my life. I'm like trying to do something constructive with it, you know? Jeannie and Didi think this is hilarious. They do this choirgirl thing where they both fold their hands like they're praying and hum "Amazing Grace," which is what we do when somebody starts to get religious on us. Then, just to be complete assholes, they sing, *Alison, we know this world is killing you . . .* et cetera, which is kind of like my theme song when I'm being a drag.

So I go:

*They say you're nothing but party girls*
*Just like a million more all over the world*

They crack up. We all love Costello.

After they finally leave, I open up my script but I'm

having trouble concentrating, it's this play called *Mourning Becomes Electra,* so I call up my little sister at home. Of course the line is busy and they don't have call waiting so I call the operator and request an emergency breakthrough on the line. I listen while the operator cuts in. I hear Carol's voice and then the operator says there's an emergency call from Vanna White in New York. Carol immediately says Alison, in this moaning, grown-up voice even though she's three years younger than me.

What's new? I go when she gets rid of the other call.

Same old stuff, she says. Mom's drunk. My car's in the shop. Mickey's out on bail. He's drunk, too.

Listen, do you know where Dad is? I go and she says, Virgin Islands last she heard, maybe St. Croix but she doesn't have a number either. So I tell her about my school thing and then maybe because I'm feeling a little weird about it I tell her about Skip, except I say five hundred dollars instead of a thousand, and she says it sounds like he totally deserved it. He's such a prick, I go, and Carol says, yeah, he sounds just like Dad.

And I go, yeah, just like.

Jeannie comes back Sunday morning at 9:00 A.M. She's a shivering wreck. For a change I'm just waking up instead of just going to sleep. I give Jeannie a Valium and put her to bed. It's sort of a righteous feeling, being on this end of the whole experience—I feel like a doctor or something.

She lies in bed stiff as a mannequin and says, I'm so afraid, Alison. She is not a happy unit.

We're all afraid, I go.

In half an hour she's making these horrible chainsaw sleep noises.

Thanks to Skip, Monday morning I'm at school doing dance and voice. Paid my bill in cash. Now I'm feeling great. Really good. In the afternoon I've got acting class. We start with sense-memory work. I sit down in class and my teacher tells me I'm at a beach. He wants me to see the sand and the water and feel the sun on my bare skin. Hear the volleyballs whizzing past. No problem. First I have to clear myself out. That's part of the process. All around me people are making strange noises, stretching, getting their yayas out, preparing for their own exercises. Some people I swear, even though this is supposed to be totally spontaneous, you can always tell some of these people are acting for the teacher even in warm-up, laughing or crying so dramatically, like, *look at me, I'm so spontaneous.* There's a lot of phonies in this profession. Anyway, I don't know—I'm just letting myself go limp in the head, then I'm laughing hysterically and next thing I'm bawling like a baby, really out of control, falling out of my chair and thrashing all over the floor . . . a real basket case . . . epileptic apocalypse, sobbing and flailing around, trying to take a bite out of the linoleum . . . they're used to some pretty radical emoting in here, but this is way over the top, apparently. I kind of lose it, and the nurse says I'm overtired and tells me to go home and rest. . . .

That night my old man finally calls. I'm like, I must be dreaming.

Pissed at you, I go, when he asks how I am.

I'm sorry, honey, he says, about the tuition. I screwed up.

You're goddamn right you did, I say.

Oh, baby, he goes, I'm a mess.

You're telling me, I go.

He says, she left me.

Don't come crying to me about what's-her-name, I say. Then he starts to whine and I go, when are you going to grow up, for Christ's sake?

I bitch him out for a while and then I tell him I'm sorry, it's okay, he's well rid of her, there's lots of women who would love a sweet man like him. Not to mention his money. Story of his life. But I don't say that of course. He's fifty-two years old and it's a little late to teach him the facts of life. From what I've seen nobody changes much after a certain age. Like about four years old, maybe. Anyway, I hold his hand and cool him out and almost forget to hit him up for money.

He promises to send me the tuition and the rent and something extra. I'm not holding my breath.

I should hate my father, sometimes I think I do. There was a girl in the news the last few weeks, she hired her boyfriend to shoot her old man. Families, Jesus. At least with lovers you can break up. These old novels and plays that always start out with orphans, in the end they find their parents—I want to say, don't look for them, you're better off without. Believe me. Get a dog instead. That's one of my big ambitions in life—to be an orphan. With a trust fund, of course. And a harem of men to come and go as I command, guys as beautiful and faceless as the men who lay you down in your dreams.

# 2 SCENES FOR ONE MAN AND ONE WOMAN

Watch out! Rebecca's coming to town, and I'm definitely not talking about the one from Sunnybrook Farm. This is my maniac sister. She's flying in from Palm Beach with her latest squeeze, staying at the Stanhope. If I was the management at that establishment I'd hide all the valuables, tie everything else down and stretch a tarp over it. Last time she was in New York they actually threw her out of the Sherry Netherland, and Rod Stewart and his band used to practically live at that dump. Like, I'm sure those guys behaved themselves, right?—TVs out the windows, groupies out the wazoo. . . . So you can imagine what my sister can do to a room. Becca uses things up quickly—cars, credit cards, men, drugs, horses, you name it. The men and the credit cards are sort of mixed up together—after she's totally burned out some guy she usually asks if she can have a credit card which he'll wait for five days and then report stolen. I don't know, she must give great head is all I can say because these guys always say yes, even when she's done something really horrible like sleep with their best friend. The best way I can think of to describe Rebecca is to say she's like the Tasmanian Devil, that character in the Bugs Bunny cartoons that moves around inside a tornado and demolishes everything in his path. Or else she's like an entire heavy metal band on tour—all wrapped up in this cute little hundred-and-ten-pound package.

What really worries me is the combination of Becca and Didi. When those two get together it's like—what were the two things you were never supposed to mix in chemistry class or you'd like blow up the whole school? You know what I mean. Not oil and water—something else. So much for my education. Blanks that never got filled in. None of the above. Story of my life. Anyway, I know several drug dealers who are going to open bottles of Cristal and buy new Ferraris when they hear that Becca's back in town—I'm talking about guys who bought their *first* Ferraris out of profits from Didi's trust fund—but for the rest of us it's basically like hearing that a hurricane's cruising across the Gulf toward your brand-new uninsured beach house. Just when I was getting my acting together.

But the main thing is I've met a guy and I'm totally in lust, so who cares about Rebecca? What's really amazing is that his mind is what I was attracted to first, and I wasn't even thinking about the other thing.

# STORY OF MY LIFE

I'm at Nell's, as usual, hanging out. Me, Didi, Jeannie, Rebecca and my friend Francesca, who I haven't mentioned yet—she's practically my best friend, we used to show horses together, no one else could stand her because she was Super-JAP, her Dad's a big movie producer and her mother is some sort of Rockefeller, so she had a stableful of the best hunters and jumpers in the country, she was always throwing tantrums and screaming at the judges and the other girls but we got along great from the word go, and now she supposedly works for William Morris although I've never been able to reach her there. She has one of those incredible jobs that you just hate the people who luck into them, the kind of job I'd have to have if I was ever going to become a member of the work force. So she works for William Morris, but when I say *works* I'm being a major philanthropist. I mean, she gets this job as an assistant to a high-powered agent and the next week her boss gets diagnosed with AIDS and of course everyone is totally sympathetic and enlightened—I mean, come on—so of course the agency keeps him on even though he's in the hospital half of the time and three-quarters of his clients bail out for ICM and CAA and Triad, so all Francesca has to do is show up once in a while and answer letters of condolence. But meantime she's got this sort of credibility and access from being with William Morris, not to mention being her father's daughter.

So Francesca, she knows everyone, right? Partly because of her family and also because that's her great passion in life, meeting rich and famous people. A lot of people think she's a snob or a starfucker because all she can talk about is lunch with Jack Nicholson and drinks with Sting, but she's so up front about it you can't hold it against her, really. She's totally wide-eyed, which is pretty amazing given her background: all these famous people always coming over to the house for dinner, you'd think she'd get jaded, but she'll walk across the room to meet a guy who had a walk-on in "The Young and the Restless," congratulate him on his career. Granted, it's a little bit *too* much sometimes—like, Francesca, I'd like you to meet Adolf Hitler, and she'd be like—oh, wow, I just loved your last war. Her ambition in life is to get invited to Mick and Jerry's house for dinner. She keeps cultivating people who know them and saying nice things in public about Mick's music and Jerry's legs and even *I* want to puke sometimes when I'm around her. But basically she's totally cool and would do anything for me or any of her friends.

So we're sitting on one of those supposedly antique couches at Nell's and I have to go to the bathroom—no, honestly. It's wall-to-wall people so while I'm waiting for this path to clear this guy says to me, didn't I see you on stage in Williamstown last summer?

And I'm like, sure.

He goes, in *The Seagull,* right? Wasn't that you?

And I go, I wish.

He looks real young—I mean he looks my age, boyish. Blondish hair that needs a trim, white sneakers, blue jeans, white shirt, this old ratty blazer that fits him like a bathrobe. Eyes like the Caribbean, warm and blue green.

So I go, if you want to meet me, just say so.

And he says, you are an actress, aren't you?

And I say, how can you tell?

I don't know, he says, the way you carry yourself.

It's called a Maidenform underwire, I go, because that's where he's looking.

God bless the manufacturer, he says. I'll buy some of their stock tomorrow.

I like the way he raises his eyebrows and the corners of his lips when he says this.

So I look down at his crotch and say, you'd be better off buying stock in Levi Strauss. Looks like it's going up.

I kind of hope they might come down, actually, he says.

And I go, suit yourself, there's no law against self-abuse.

He doesn't have a snappy comeback for that one. Most guys can't really go the distance. But still, he's cute.

So really, I say, how'd you know I'm an actress? I'm thinking, maybe my training is starting to show, I know my voice is a lot less nasal than it used to be, at least some of the time, my voice teacher says I've got to work my voice down into my chest—it'll have a lot more room down there, he goes, he's sort of a dirty old man, but cool. Plus I'm working on my posture. My mom used to actually try to get us to walk around the house balancing a book on the top of our heads, that's so typical of her, we'd be like, right, sure Mom, pass the Doritos and turn up the volume on your way out—that's probably the only thing anybody in my house ever thought of doing with a book so naturally I'm impressed by guys who actually read some. But I kind of wish I'd listened to my mom about posture, I'm like the hunchback of Seventy-eighth Street and now I have to improve my posture for my acting career. Anyway, I'm asking him how he knew I was an actress.

I guess I'm just incredibly perceptive, he says.

I go, am I supposed to believe that?

Also I overheard you talking to your friends, he says.

You've been eavesdropping, I say. Actually, I'm kind of

flattered. Usually when I'm out with Didi it's hard to get any attention. Plus I like the fact that he's honest enough to admit the real story—if there's one thing I hate it's the usual bullshit.

He tells me his name is Dean Chasen and I tell him mine is Alison Poole. I mean, that's a sign right there—if I have any doubts about a guy I just give him a bogus name.

Dean's waiting for me when I come out of the bathroom, so I let him buy me a drink. Francesca and Didi are waving and pointing from the other end of the room but I ignore them, I'm into what Dean is saying, it turns out he knows everything about theater, even though he's a Wall Streeter, sells bonds or something. We start talking about all the plays around town and he asks me about my classes and then we have this debate about method versus other kinds of training, when he first came to New York he studied at the Neighborhood Playhouse for a while under Meisner. He's thirty-two, it turns out, but he seems a lot younger. He says he wants to retire at the age of thirty-five and write plays, maybe novels.

It's a funny thing but I've noticed when I'm with creative guys like artists and actors, they hardly ever talk about their work, they're always talking about the stock market or something like they're trying to convince you they understand the real world, then you get with stockbrokers and bankers and all they want to talk about is art and the theater and they practically apologize for making a lot of money.

Usually when I meet a guy it takes me about three seconds to wonder how big his dick is. Didi and Jeannie swear by the hand method—you know: big hands, big dick—

but I was so into just talking to Dean and listening to him that it was like hours before it even occurred to me to notice he had these long, delicate hands, and after the first night I slept with him I called Didi up right away and said thin fingers don't always mean what you think.

We just start talking like we've known each other all our lives. Dean notices a lot of stuff, he has this really interesting way of looking at the world—for instance, they have this real good DJ at Nell's and he was spinning some weird oldies in with the new stuff and suddenly Dean says, you know, 'Lightning Striking Again' is the only song that actually *features* the backup vocals.

So I say, I like the line, *I can't stop now, I can't stop,* that could be my theme.

Anyway, Dean just notices these funny little things. I like that. In some ways he's like a five-year-old boy practically. When I told him he was like a little kid he says, Alison, we're a nation of children. I love the way he comes up with stuff like that. I mean, I was just talking about him but he turns it into something about the world.

The next thing I know we're at his apartment, still talking. It's like we're a dialogue machine or something. I tell him about my old boyfriends and that I've slept with thirty-six guys and I go, how about you?

He goes, none, totally deadpan.

And I go, don't give me that.

And he goes, honest, no guys. Cracked me up.

He tells me about Patty, this girl he just broke up with after two years. He still loves her, he says, but basically he doesn't like her, she wants to get married and move to the suburbs and he's not ready for that. So they broke up about a month ago. I tell him he doesn't seem like the suburban type and he says, really.

Sometimes I feel like I'm stuck between being my father and being some kind of animal, he goes. What I do for a living—don't get me wrong, I like it and it's challenging as hell, but it's so conventional I feel like I have stay up all night and beat myself up just so I know I'm still alive. He says, in a few years I'm going to quit and just do what I want to do.

So fine, I say, who's stopping you?

I'm afraid I'll stop myself, he goes. I'm afraid I'll get fat and complacent in the meantime.

I'll call you in three years and remind you, I say.

If the markets hold up, he says, I'll have a million and then some by then. This starving artist thing, I don't think it's entirely necessary, you know? If I can put some money away I think I'll be able to really concentrate on writing a lot better than if I'm working as a messenger, he says.

Absolutely, I go, but I'm thinking, I don't know, how many great writers worked on Wall Street for half their lives then suddenly started cranking out the old masterpieces? I mean, I like this guy a lot, but my brain is still functioning, okay?

So then we talk all about drama and he keeps jumping up to pull books off the shelves and read me bits, he's got like about eight walls of books, his living room looks like the public library or something.

Finally when the birds start squawking outside he says, you want to stay over? and I'm, like, sure, why not? Here we are having this great conversation, but I'm also thinking, here's this guy I really like and respect, maybe I shouldn't fuck him. You know, it's been so long since I've met a guy who isn't a total asshole that I forget what the rules are. Then I remember about Skip's little present. The doctor told me two weeks and it's only been about a week since I started taking the pills and I still feel a little itchy. And it's weird but all of sudden now that I can't fuck him I really want to, and for a minute I consider taking my chances. But that would be a really shitty thing to do, so I explain the situation and he's really sweet about it. We'll just have to wait, he says.

Easier said than done. First we're just kissing, and then he touches my breast, and that's the road to trouble. My left nipple in particular. If you want to get Alison all hot and bothered that's the button to press. After an hour of touching and kissing and rubbing I'm going out of my mind. Dean brings me off with his hand but it's just not the same, I want more, I don't want to stop.

Poor Dean is like, dying of a monster hard-on. After a couple of hours it feels like something carved out of stone and heated over the fire. I'm wondering if maybe I should help him out a little but I think oral sex on the first date is pretty rude, like I'm almost always turned off when some guy I hardly know goes down on me. Under the circumstances I should do something for Dean but the thing is, I really want him inside me.

Please, I go. Please. He's on top of me, kissing and dry humping.

Alison, he moans. Don't.

I can't stand it, I go.

I can't either.

Goddamn Skip Pendleton, I go.

Skip Pendleton? he says, lifting his head from my shoulder.

You know him? I say.

He's like, he's a friend of mine.

Small world, I say.

Dean goes, he was the one who gave you this . . . disease?

I think so.

You *think* so?

I can tell Dean's a little bummed out about this. He kind of rolls away, and even though he tells me it's fine, he didn't know me then, I can tell he has that whole male competitive thing. Men don't want women unless they've been wanted by other men, they're not interested if you're not desirable to their friends. But then they expect you to have resisted all the interest until they came along. I guess it's because he knows Skip. The idea of the other thirty-five didn't seem to bother him too much.

Suddenly, out of the blue, he says, don't you ever worry about, you know, AIDS?

I say, sure, I worry, but I think it's been blown out of proportion. I try to be careful who I sleep with.

Like Skip? he says. That fucking guy is a walking petri dish.

I'm like, I thought you said he was your friend.

The next day, actually the same day, I wake up at one in the afternoon. I try to remember if I have class, what day is it. Dean isn't in bed. I smell coffee but I don't hear anything. I figure maybe he's gone to work, but then I hear him moving around out in the next room. There's a phone next to the bed so I dial Francesca.

Tell me everything, she goes. I want details. Length, width, position and duration.

I go, you got your computer booted?

Francesca enters all of her conquests on her computer with detailed notes about their performance plus she has separate files for the sex adventures of her friends.

I explain the problem to her. She's already heard about my social disease, must be everybody's favorite subject this week.

Well, she says, at least you gave him a blow job, I hope.

I go, actually I didn't.

Alison! What's the matter with you? Don't you like him? It's the least you can do after getting the poor guy all hot and then telling him you caught some slimy social disease from his best friend. You're really slipping.

After that I call my apartment to talk to Jeannie. My sister Rebecca answers the phone. She sounds crazed, which is a big surprise.

What are you doing there? I go and she goes, after we left Nell's we went over to Emile's house and bought a quarter and we're just trying to finish it up.

I'm like, it's two in the afternoon, for Christ's sake. Most normal people have already been to sleep at least once already.

Did you get laid? Rebecca wants to know.

Then Didi comes on the line. She screams, you better have since you ditched your best friends. Then in a pretty normal voice, if anybody who's been up all night drinking, smoking and doing coke can have a normal voice, she says, come over and help us finish this quarter ounce.

Where's Jeannie? I go, and Didi says, Jeannie passed

out in the bedroom around five and went in to work at nine.

I'm worried about Jeannie because she's the only one of us who actually has a job and at this rate she won't have it long. It's hard to concentrate when you hang around with us.

After trying unsuccessfully to find my old man, who still hasn't come through with a check, the son of a bitch, I get up and go into the other room, but first I look around for something to wear, being the incredibly modest girl that I am. In his closet he's got about twenty shirts and I pick out a blue Oxford from Brooks Brothers. I approve. When I was thirteen I started wearing my father's Brooks Brothers and now my standard outfit is one of those big old fat businessmen's shirts—sixteen and a half thirty-four, untucked of course—leggings, white socks and sneakers or loafers.

The door to the bathroom is open and the water's running. I kind of peek in. I'm a little worried about what kind of mood he'll be in. Dean's shaving, so cute in his plaid boxer shorts, and he's using one of those old-fashioned safety razors, the kind I remember Pops using—that's my grandfather. He has one of those shaving brushes all lathered up beside the sink and it's weird, I have this kind of déjà vu of being a really tiny girl and waking up real early one morning in Gran and Pop's house in Palm Beach and following the sound of running water to Pop's bathroom where he was shaving just like this. He let me watch and I was so impressed, like I was witnessing some religious ceremony. This was like, prehistoric times, before Mom and Dad got divorced.

Good morning, I go, and Dean looks over, says good morning. He's smiling even though you can tell he doesn't want to. He tries to swallow the smile, remember that he's mad at me.

So how are you this morning, I go, and he says fine.

Did you blow off work, I ask, and he says he called in and said he was taking the day off, he had one coming. He says it like he wants me to think he was planning all along to take the day off, as if it had nothing to do with me or staying up all night.

And I go, I didn't know people still used those kind of razors.

And he says, I guess I'm an old-fashioned guy.

And I go, that's cool, I like that.

And he goes, oh yeah? I'm surprised.

Why are you so surprised, I say.

And he says, I think of you as a postmodern girl.

I don't know if this is a compliment or what, it doesn't really sound like it, but just to clear the air I go, sorry about last night.

And he says, what's to be sorry for?

And I say, you're probably a little horny.

I'll live, he goes.

Jesus, men can be so silly when they think they're being macho and tough. Sometimes I think there must be some kind of secret ritual like circumcision where all boys have three-quarters of their brain removed at adolescence, or else they just have to promise that they'll act and talk like they've been lobotomized, grunt in monosyllables like cavemen, and limit their emotions to the range between A and B. Still, they're the only other sex we've got. And they can make you feel so good sometimes you want to scream like the housewife who's just won the big prize on "Wheel of Fortune" and generally forgive them for being men.

So Dean finishes shaving, wipes himself off and walks out into the kitchen, ignoring me. I follow him in. Cute butt. He sits down at the table and picks up the *Times.*

I'm thinking about firing up the first cigarette of the day but then I get another idea.

Poor baby didn't get no satisfaction, I say, coming up behind him and rubbing the back of his neck. I start singing, I can't get no . . . I can't get no . . .

He resists for a while, keeping the muscles tense as I work my way down, pretending he's reading, but gradually he starts to slump in his chair and when I kneel down in front of him and start to massage the inside of his legs he lets out this big moan. He reaches out to stroke my hair, leans his head back, closes his eyes, his breath catching in his throat when I reach for the little opening in his boxers.

He gasps when I take him inside my mouth, and that's just the beginning. I mean, I haven't met too many guys who say *no thanks, honey, I'd rather watch the game* when you suggest a blow job. But still, I never heard anything like the chorus of weird satisfied sounds coming from Dean while I'm going down on him. It makes me feel really good, like a nurse or maybe an angel, doing my good deed for the day. I mean, this boy is appreciative and that really inspires me.

What can I say? I'm an actress.

Let me just say that in general my feeling about blow jobs is, I can take them or leave them. In fact, mainly I could leave them. Guys, of course, won't let you and I suppose you can't blame them. I mean, if it's anything like having a guy you really like go down on you, particularly if he's shaved recently, then who can hold it against them, really? God knows I'd rather lose my left arm than go without that for the rest of my life. So, like, I usually figure its kind of a trade-off. You know, the I'll-lick-yours-if-you'll-lick-mine kind of thing. Except one thing that really grosses me out—somebody ought to write a book about modern etiquette that covers this sort of thing—one thing I hate, right? is some guy going down on me the first date. I think that's incredibly presumptuous and rude. Fucking is one thing. But sticking your face in someone's crotch—I mean, that's really intimate. And I get really uncomfortable and weirded out when it's some guy whose name I never did catch over the music on the dance floor. I think you should put some talking and kissing mileage on your lips before you put them on my, uh, lips. Okay, guys? Just in case anybody out there wants to know.

And another thing I don't like, as long as we're on the subject, is when some guy is going down on you, and you're like—wow, even if there isn't a God it's okay, I can deal with it no problem, like, I could give a shit—and you're floating in some kind of warm liquid trance when you suddenly feel the old pivot. You know what I mean, the old swivel where he's still got his tongue in your southern cleavage but it's rotating, swinging the hips northward and suddenly there's this dick banging against your teeth. I don't know, I suppose trading favors is what it's all about. I mean sometimes I think we're all just masturbating each other any way you look at it. If we're not jerking each other around, we're jerking each other off. But still, do we have to be so blatant about it? I mean, *really.*

Actually, my last real boyfriend, Alex—the only real boyfriend I ever had in my life, we went out for five years—he was blatant about it. He'd make deals. Like, for instance, I'd be looking through the new Saks catalogue that just arrived in the mail and I'd point to a sweater or something and say, I love that, and he'd go, I'll get it for you and I'd go, really? and he'd be like raising his eyebrows and winking. And I'd be like, oh, yeah, I get it.

So I'd get tough and make him fill out the order form with his credit card number and seal the envelope before I'd go down on him. And when I was really being a hard-ass I'd make him walk it out to the post office with his hard-on. I don't know, I think it turned him on even more. The harder a time I'd give him, the harder he'd be.

Alex was really pissed when I read in *Vogue* or somewhere that there's like twelve hundred calories or something like that in an average load of come. Because at the time I was kind of anorexic and the last thing I was looking for was a way to swallow an extra thousand-plus calories. So I got kind of reluctant after that. Because, really, it seems to me it's kind of rude and insulting not to swallow. Like inviting someone to your house for a dinner party and then making them eat in the kitchen with the help. Anyway, God was Alex pissed. I think he even wrote a letter to the editor of *Vogue.* Or maybe it was *Cosmo.* Whatever. He got paranoid and started talking about feminist dykes taking over the media and stuff. And when he wanted it he'd whine and squirm like a hound with his nose in a foxhole, because as I say I wasn't that hot on the whole operation to begin with. When you love someone, okay. I loved Alex, and there is some kind of special thing about doing something for someone you love that's a better feeling than anything else in the world, even if it's something you normally wouldn't do at all. Or maybe especially if it's something you normally wouldn't do.

Did I say love? Wash my mouth out with soap. Dean said this great thing last night, we were talking about drama, and Dean quotes this line, it goes, men have died from time to time and worms have eaten them, but not for love. And I'm like, absolutely. It's from Shakespeare, a girl called Rosalind says it. Dean says I remind him of Rosalind, says she's a great character. So maybe I'll check out this play, see if it's got a monologue I can use.

Anyway . . . I wonder sometimes if it would have lasted with Alex if he hadn't fucked me over. Then I say—what are you, soft in the head? It never lasts. I haven't seen one example yet. But there's still this ideal in your head, you know, like a vision of a place you've never visited, but that you've dreamed about or seen in a movie you've forgotten the title of, and you know you'd recognize it immediately if you ever saw it in real life. It would be like going home, tired and whipped after a really long time on the road, if home was like it's supposed to be, instead of the disaster area it actually is.

# 3 SENSE-MEMORY

So I kiss Dean good-bye about three in the afternoon.

Can you taste yourself? I go, and he blushes. I swear, these older guys are so straight. Cracks me up. You'd think growing up in the sixties when everybody was balling at rock festivals and doing acid would've made them pretty wild, but most of the guys I know who are around thirty—they shock pretty easily. I don't know, maybe it's just me. Am I so outspoken? All my friends are like this, so how weird can I be? But I think with a little work we might be able to loosen old Dean up. He's definitely got potential.

Anyway, Dean, he's wearing this shit-eating grin on his face which he's had ever since I came up for air, which is a good thing, I'm glad he's happy, since I have to ask him for cab money because I've got to get back to my apartment to change and pick up my script and then downtown to Strasberg within the hour. I hate to start right in hitting him up for money but he's real sweet about it and gives me a twenty and I kiss him again and before we know it we're both getting into it again and it looks like school may be out the window, but then I remember my little problem, plus the phone rings so we both step back gasping for air and he goes, I'll call you—his voice all sexy like it's been smoked and sandpapered, then doused in hot pepper sauce—and I go, you better.

Not that I wouldn't call him. I will if I want, when I want. I hate waiting for anything, including for the phone to ring. Why wait? is my motto. I don't understand these girls who think the guy has to call them, like its some kind of deviant behavior for females to touch the push buttons on a phone. *Ooh, icky. I couldn't possibly!* My mother was always like that. Even after I know she's screwing the pool man, she has these little formulas for ladylike behavior she picked up at Miss Porter's or someplace—*a lady never calls a gentleman.* Probably wears white gloves when she gives a hand job.

My mother. She called last night just before I went out to dinner wanting to talk about her boyfriend. Carl owns a construction company supposedly and she's trying to decide whether she should break up with him since he's shiftless and lazy—those are her words, she talks like a plantation belle—but she's been trying to decide for five years. Anyway, it gives her something to think about besides Dad. She used to do charity work and paint watercolors, really beautiful landscapes, at least I thought they were really beautiful when I was a kid, I used to love to watch her paint out on the sunporch, we had this great house on Long Island when I was a kid and my parents were still married, I loved all the shades of blue in her paint set, these blue disks that between them contained all the moods of the sky and the ocean. But the pictures got smaller and smaller until they were about the size of postage stamps, she was using these brushes with one bristle, painting transparent mountains the size of pimples, then she stopped completely. I think it was Dad making fun of her that did it. Every time she tried to do something it was a joke. From what I can tell, now she just watches the religious shows on TV and drinks wine all day. This is someone who wouldn't think of carrying a handbag that wasn't made out of alligator or wearing a party dress twice but she's buying Gallo Chablis by the gallon. Finally I got sick of hearing about Carl so I told her I'd call her later. My opinion of Carl, if you really want to know, is that the best thing that could happen to Mom is if some of his nice associates in the so-called construction business would dress him up in a cement wet suit and send him scuba diving without a tank.

Down on the street I get a cab driven by a crazy Russian. He wants to tell me the story of his life, starting with the fact that he's Caucasian.

I White Russian, he says. White!

Hey, I can see that already. It's kind of racist to keep insisting on it, if you ask me. I don't know, maybe he wants me to think they named the drink after him or something. Every ten seconds or so he rolls down the window to spit whenever he wants to show what he thinks of Communism. At least I think that's the idea. I kind of hug the right side of the cab so I don't catch any of the spray.

In America, he goes, you eat caviar for breakfast every morning if you are wanting. (I bet this is news to the girls in the typing pool.) He goes, not so Russia. (Window down—hock, spit!)

Then he goes, what do you do, fashion model?

I go, I'm an actress.

Oh yes, he goes. Movies. I know. *The West Side Story.*

That's a good one, I go.

You ever come to Brighton Beach, you look up me, the Russian says when he lets me off in front of my apartment.

And I'm like, is that in the Hamptons, or what? Never heard of it. Then I ask him if he'll wait and he goes sure.

In the elevator I'm hoping Didi and Rebecca won't be there, or at least that they'll be asleep. It's kind of hard to get started on your day when a couple of vampires have taken over your apartment. At the door I hear these weird Oriental voices coming from inside. It sounds like group therapy for giant insects.

I almost gag on the cigarette smoke and cocaine sweat when I open the door. When my eyes adjust to the dark I see them huddled on the couch, Rebecca in her leopard body stocking and Didi in the same leggings and sweatshirt she's been sporting for the last couple of weeks.

You scared the shit out of us, Little Sis, Rebecca goes.

Did you bring any beer? Didi says.

How about cigarettes? says Rebecca. We *need* cigarettes.

You need professional help, I go.

Didi goes, you bring any blow?

There's still about a gram here, Rebecca says to Didi.

And Didi goes, that's good. Are you sure?

So Rebecca says, I think so. I don't know. Maybe it's

only about seven-eighths of a gram. Or three-quarters. I don't know.

God, that's not very much, Didi goes.

And Becca goes, well, maybe nine-tenths.

And I'm like, fun with fractions. Actually, Becca was really good in school, not that she ever went, but one time they tied her down long enough to give her an IQ test and then told Mom and Dad she was a genius. Becca never let us forget it. She decided it meant that she didn't have to bother going to school or do anything that required any effort at all, ever again.

We have to call Emile and get more, says Didi, suddenly panicked.

I love coke conversations. They're so enlightening. I mean, do I sound like that? It's almost enough to make you swear off drugs forever.

The place is a real sty, beer and wine bottles all over the place, and for some reason about half of Jeannie's wardrobe is scattered around the room, plus there's like this residue of cigarette ash and cocaine on everything. The air reminds me of Mexico City, totally unbreathable. I go into my room to change.

Tell us about your new stud, Rebecca shouts from the living room.

We want details, Didi says. Length and width.

The next minute, Rebecca says, Alison, do you have any Valium? That's the good part about dealing with coke monsters. If you don't like the topic of conversation, just wait a minute and you'll get a new one. On the other hand, it never really changes at all. It's like a perpetual motion thing. The topic is always drugs.

When I leave they're calling the deli to order beer and cigarettes, Becca holding the receiver between her shoulder and her cheek while she goes down on the mirror.

Do they sell Valium? Didi goes.

Does who sell Valium? says Becca and then she goes, hello, who is this?

And Didi goes, who are you talking to? Then she seems to realize that I'm leaving. She gets real indignant. Sit down, she says. You have to help us finish this coke. You can't go anywhere until it's gone.

Didi is so bossy when she's wired. She insists that everybody else get fucked up too, plus she directs the conversation. Usually she gets away with it since she's the one who paid for the coke, plus everybody has this kind of awe of her, she's sort of a prodigy, like a crazy person. But I'm not buying it today.

Alison, she screams. Come back here. You can't go.

So then I remember this thing in my purse, it's like a business card from this drug counseling program, Jeannie gave it to me as a joke one night, actually one morning after we'd been up all night—somebody at work gave it to her and they weren't kidding. So I open my purse, fish through my wallet, all these scraps of paper, napkins with guys' phone numbers, and I find this thing, it says, MESSED UP? STRUNG OUT? NEED HELP? DIAL 555-HELP.

I go, Didi, I got a present for you. And I give her the card.

And she's like, Alison, you bitch, come back here, as I'm cruising out the door.

I'll visit you in the hospital, I say.

* * *

Didi would make a really good dictator of a Third World country. She absolutely has to be the boss and the center of attention. If someone's talking about something she's not interested in she shouts, boring! and changes the subject to something more interesting, like herself for instance. Somehow she pulls it off. Partly because she's gorgeous. Partly because at most social events she's the one with the most blow, and she uses it like a carrot and a stick. She'll sit there in the middle of the floor with her big white bag and she'll let people drool while she chops really painstaking lines or just yaks on and on as if she's oblivious to what everyone's really concentrating on, except of course she's not. She just likes to torture people. That's the carrot part. If she thinks you want it she'll keep you hanging on, like the Supremes say. But at the end of the night when your nose is bleeding and you're dying to go home and sleep, she'll demand that you do these huge lines that would choke an industrial-strength vacuum cleaner. And when you say, no way Didi, I gotta split, she'll get real indignant and go, after all this free blow I gave you, you're just going to walk out on me?

The classic story about Didi is that she makes her boyfriends change the channels when they're having sex.

I've totally forgotten about the Russian, who's been sitting there in the cab for about fifteen minutes. I feel really bad about it, poor guy probably had his fill of waiting in Russia, standing in those incredible lines for his ration of rotten groceries and stuff, actually it sounds like New York now that I think about it, but still, I have to get cigarettes, we're talking absolute necessities here, so I tell him two more minutes and I zip around the corner to the deli.

Pack of Merits, I say to the old fart behind the counter.

Hard or soft? he says, smirking.

Hard, I tell him. You know I like it hard.

The old guy cracks up. He never gets enough of this joke.

Coming out of the store I get caught in this horrible preteen pedestrian traffic jam from the school down the street. Gremlins. I practically get run over by this tiny kid with a T-shirt that says REALITY IS AN ILLUSION PRODUCED BY ALCOHOL DEFICIENCY.

Where was Planned Parenthood when we really needed them? is what I want to know.

The cabbie is cool. He's been grooving on some funky ethnic-type music on the radio—dueling balalaikas or something. You never know how many kinds of music there are in the world until you move to New York and start taking cabs. It's like, from your apartment to Trader Vic's you get Cuban music, and then from Trader Vic's to Canal Bar you've got Zorba the Greek music and then Indian ragas from Canal Bar to Nell's, Scandinavian heavy metal on the way from Nell's up to Emile's apartment. After that you start singing the Colombian national anthem.

I ask him if I can smoke and he says, not problem. And I'm like, this cab should be a national historic landmark or something, the last taxi in New York City without a No Smoking sign.

So we're cruising downtown and the Russian's telling

me the story of his life, the short version. I can't understand all of it, with the music and his accent and all, but the climax of the story is his first visit to an American supermarket after he's finally gotten an exit visa and split the Motherland. Or is it the Fatherland? Anyway, whichever, according to what this guy tells me, having Russia for your parentland proves my theory that it's better to be an orphan. So when he first gets to the old U S of A he goes to this supermarket in Brooklyn and can't believe what he sees, all the aisles of food and stuff. What really flips him out is the meat counter. He looks at all this red meat under plastic and he goes to his cousin—*Who for is all this meat?* (That's how he says it.) *Is for high officials?* he goes and his cousin goes, *It is for anyone who wants.*

I break into crying right there, the cabbie goes, to think how wonderful it is, all that meat in nice plastic for all the people who want.

I don't know, I'm going to ask him if there was a special sale that day, free meat for the masses, but I feel like a cynic. So then I feel sort of guilty and touched, you know, I'm so spoiled and this guy can weep at the sight of a pork chop. So when he asks me for my phone number as he's dropping me off I almost give it to him, but then I say, sorry, I've got a boyfriend, which is sort of true in a way. Maybe. I hope. But I like this guy, he's nice, so I don't do what I usually do which is to give him the number of the Midnite Escort Service. I just say, maybe next time.

My first class is dance, then voice. My voice teacher gets ticked off at me because I'm not concentrating. I keep talking through my nose, it's a big problem with me, and he says, what are you thinking about?

I don't say anything, but I'm thinking about Dean. And it kind of pisses me off—one night with this guy and he's distracting me from my acting. This is one of the reasons I don't believe in relationships. Who needs the distraction? But probably it's just lack of sleep. Being tired always makes me sentimental. Like when I'm really hung over I can turn on the radio and start bawling at the lyrics to some stupid song, even if it's a song I really hate. Or, you know, after a really hard night I'll pick up the *Post* and read about some hero who saved a puppy from drowning and I'll want to write him a letter and offer to marry him or have his children or something. Not that I actually do it, you know, but I think about it.

I've got this theory that the brain is sort of like $H_2O$—it's got a bunch of states. When you've been exercising and going to class and generally being a good girl the brain is a solid and it makes the right decisions. But when you've been out all night trashing yourself with alcohol and controlled substances, or sometimes when you're having really great sex, your gray matter turns to mush and your judgment turns to shit. You know, right in the middle of a good orgasm you'll go completely liquid and for a while afterward you'll think about true love and marriage and other, like, ancient myths.

Finally voice is over and I go to my acting class, which is usually my best. The sensory exercise for the week is sharp taste. Our teacher, Rob, gives us a little pep talk first about how we really have to taste it, and it should be clear to anybody watching us, say, from across a restaurant, that we're experiencing this sharp taste. So I decide on jalapeño peppers. I'm a fiend for Mexican food, and I like it hot. I always order extra jalapeños on the side. I sometimes think I must have some kind of chemical deficiency that can only be filled with Mexican food. Not to mention margaritas. The trouble is, when you start drinking frozen margaritas, there's no telling where you'll end up, or with who.

So I start thinking about jalapeños, and everybody else in the class goes off into their thing while the teacher walks around checking us out. After ten minutes I'm like bored out of my gourd. My cheeks hurt, and my eyes feel like they're starting to grow mold they've been watery so long. The teacher asks Burt, the guy next to me, what he's tasting and he says gorgonzola cheese.

I can't see that, Rob says.

I say, thank God we can't smell it.

And Rob goes, Alison, if you were concentrating you wouldn't have even heard my remark, which is true.

Finally he can see we're all really bored with sensory so he says try something psychological over that, which is cool because that's when it gets interesting.

For example, he goes, think of something good you did for someone else that made you feel good about yourself. And put that together with sharp taste. Okay, people, he says, let's really reach down and use our instrument.

The instrument is like, all your acting skills and knowledge and talent put together, your body too but more than your body, it's not an actual thing but kind of a concept. Anyway, I think about it for a minute and then I just about die. Something good you did for someone . . . sharp taste.

They told me later that within two minutes I had the

teacher watching me and that pretty soon he told everyone else to knock off what they were doing and watch me. I don't know, I was off in my own world, acting. I'm doing something true, I know I'm not just faking it this time and even though it's acting something I'm not really experiencing it's absolutely honest, my reaction, the sensations I'm feeling and I'm completely in my own reality, it's like dreaming, you know, or like riding when you feel almost like you and your horse are the same animal, taking your best jumper over a hard course and hitting everything perfectly. . . .

Something good that I did for someone . . . sharp taste. I was combining these two incredible sensations. And I knew it was the best I had ever done. It was taking me to a place I'd never been. When I finally came out of it, everybody was looking at me.

That was wonderful, the teacher says. Very very good. You were completely in tune with your instrument. Tell us what your sensory was, Alison.

Jalapeño peppers, I say.

And he goes, what about your psychological?

You really want to know? I go.

Yes, of course, he goes.

Well, I was thinking about giving my boyfriend a blow job.

That cracks everyone up.

And I'm thinking, boyfriend? Why did I say boyfriend? What's the matter with me? I'm totally in lust. I know it will pass so I don't worry about it too much and in the meantime I got this incredible acting experience out of it. I figured out real early on that the bad stuff—all the shitty things that ever happened to you—feeds your work, I mean, the teacher says the more bad things that happen to you the better for your art, and I'm like—hey, I could be a fucking genius, but anyway, this is the first time I've made something enjoyable really work for my art, pardon the A word.

When the laughter dies down my teacher says, were you thinking of a specific instance, or just in general?

Specific, I go. Very specific. In fact it was this morning.

This cracks them all up again.

Then we get down to acting. I'm glad he liked my sense-memory because I don't have anything ready to perform. Luckily there's some eager beavers ready to strut their stuff. I don't know, you've got to be a bit of masochist to be in this class because Rob can be brutal. First this girl Janet who used to write her own material until Rob finally put a stop to that. It was pretty horrible. She gets up and says she's going to do Blanche from *Streetcar.*

Rob goes, not the kindness of strangers. I thought I told the class I didn't want anybody doing that monologue ever again.

Old Janet's standing in front of the class looking like—oh, God, why does he hate me? And I'm feeling nice and safe in my wobbly little classroom chair, thinking, better you than me, Janet.

Rob sighs and tells Janet to go ahead so she does, yada yada yada, really bad, I mean, bring back Vivien Leigh, please.

Finally Rob shouts, she's in the attic.

I don't know what it means but he always hollers this whenever he really hates something. He'll tell us the story some day, or so he says.

Janet asks, do you want me to stop?

Please, Rob says, cease and desist. Then he launches into this thing where he tears her performance apart and goes on to talk about her sex life—Rob should have been a psychotherapist. You just broke up with your boyfriend, didn't you? Rob shouts. Janet squeaks yes and then starts bawling. He gets really personal in his criticism. The roles we choose and how we perform them show a lot about us, Rob says.

And while I'm supposed to be paying attention I'm wondering what Dean is doing, if he's thinking of me. Then I think I may have to go out and screw somebody else or something just to get my sense of perspective back.

# 4 TRUTH OR DARE

After class I stop off at the tanning salon. I'm hoping Mark will be there because I'm flat broke and I used my last tanning coupon a few days ago. Luckily Mark's behind the counter but he has to give me a bunch of shit first and say if his boss catches him giving out free tans he'll be shit-canned and I have to remind him about some favors I've done for him, so he gives me my usual bed but I have to wait five minutes so I decide to call Francesca from the pay phone after I borrow a quarter from Mark.

Alison, he goes, have you ever thought of getting a job?

Not really, I go. Have you?

I've got a job, he goes.

And I go, you call this working?

If I really gave a shit what Mark thinks I could tell him I had a job once. I was a waitress for about three seconds. I don't know, it was pretty terrible, these businessmen thinking the price of their filet included a handful of ass and the manager wanted to sleep with me, plus the other waitresses weren't too keen on me since Jeannie's father owned the restaurant. Sorry, I just wasn't raised to work. I mean, you take an indoor cat eating smoked salmon and lying around in the sunny spots all its life—you can't suddenly chuck it out into the cold and expect it to feed itself and fight like an alley cat. I should start a clinic for former rich girls. Deprived Debs Anonymous.

Francesca picks up on the second ring. Tell me all, she goes. I want to know everything about Dean. I need details. Length and width, the works. Did you take my advice?

Francesca likes to pile up the questions, mainly because she hates to stop talking, she's like scared she'll have to let someone else talk the way kids are afraid of the moment when somebody notices it's their bedtime. I don't know, that sounds too negative, what it really is, she's like a force of nature, Niagara Falls or something.

I go, I took it.

And she's like, tell me all.

And I'm like, I'm not going to tell you everything. It was good, it was great, I like him. I'm in lust.

And she goes, I can't believe you're not going to tell me every little thing, your best friend, I'm so upset, at least tell me how big.

So I go, big.

And she goes, oh God, let me sit down, I'm getting dizzy, it's been so long since I've been laid two inches would feel big to me. Four inches would feel like a baseball bat. This is no fair, I have to live vicariously through your lust life and now you're holding out on me. Listen, do you know Bobby Cayman? Real dark, craggy. Looks like he just stepped off a Harley Davidson? I ran into him at Nell's after you left with what's-his-face and he is a total hunk.

Forget it, I tell her. Used to be a junkie.

Shit, why do I always go for men in the high risk categories?

It's true. Francesca only seems to like guys who look like heavy-metal lead guitarists or bikers, hunks in leather with needle tracks and dubious sexual histories, the kind of guys who are like, what is it that Dean says?—walking petri dishes for sexually transmitted diseases. Francesca could get laid a lot more often if her tastes weren't so narrow. She's real picky, but she picks badly. It's like, choosy mothers would never choose the kind of guys Francesca likes for son-in-law material. Sometimes I think she looks at a guy and goes, oh, wow! my mom would really be horrified by this stud.

It was so depressing at Nell's last night, Francesca says. There were absolutely no celebs. Plus I heard that Mick and Jerry had a dinner party and I wasn't invited again. I'm really upset at Caroline because she knows them like really well and she was there last night and she still won't introduce me.

Did I already say this is Francesca's big goal in life, to get invited to Mick and Jerry's house for dinner? I don't know what she'd have to live for if the invitation ever came. She goes on and on about this dinner party she wasn't invited to while I'm thinking I should probably get a bikini wax except I don't have any money. Plus I'm not a glutton for that kind of pain. It's not easy to bring tears to my eyes, but the old bikini wax does it every time. Underarm waxing is the worst, though. These places should hand out Demerol free of charge.

Mark tells me my bed's ready so I tell Francesca I gotta go and I'll call after I finish tanning. Then I call Jeannie collect at work.

Did you get any sleep? I go.

Hardly, she goes, and then she makes me tell her the whole story about Dean. Finally I ask her if she's checked the messages and she hasn't so I dial in and hear Francesca's voice again, plus some crazy guy named Mannie looking for Rebecca, he sounds deranged, not a stable unit, there's always some crazy guy looking for Rebecca. But no Dean.

When we went to L.A. last summer, Francesca and me, we'd catch this air-quality index on the radio. We were supposedly out there looking for jobs, right? We had this little house in Santa Monica on Second Street which was Party Central—but anyway, what was I talking about? Oh yeah, there was this radio station we listened to, and between Madonna and the Beastie Boys the DJ would be like—the air really sucks today, don't go out unless it's absolutely necessary kind of thing. I really hate Madonna but that's another story. So anyway, coming back to my apartment made me think about the air-quality index . . . don't go inside unless really you have to. Heavy smog, hydrocarbons and BO. I mean, it's never exactly a rose garden, but this is radical. Rebecca and Didi are really disgusting is all I can say. I have to open up all the windows and run the fan in the air conditioner for cross-ventilation. I don't even want to think about dealing with the ashtrays. If I'd bought stock in Philip Morris yesterday I'd probably be a rich girl today.

So I clear some space on the bed and lie down with my script for a half an hour or so but the next thing I know the phone is ringing and I've been asleep and I'm listening to my message going—hi, this is Alison, Jeannie and I aren't home right now, so leave the data and we'll call you lata.

So I pick up and it's Dean.

He goes, hey, how's my little postmodern girl?

I'm spacey, I go.

By definition, he goes. So what are you doing? he says.

I think I was just having an erotic dream, I tell him, because it's just coming back to me.

Was I in it? he goes and I'm thinking, for a supposedly smart guy Dean can be pretty predictable. I could lie, of course, and say he was but I feel really strongly about always being honest no matter what. That's my personal code, basically— do anything you'd be willing to admit, and always tell the truth. I don't know, though, that thing about Skip, telling him I was preggers, it's been bugging me. It's the first time in years I can remember that I've lied, but we were talking survival. And revenge, which is a girl's best friend.

So when Dean wants to know is he in my stupid dream, I go, I'm not sure, because I'm not. I don't think it was any guy in particular. Maybe if I went right back to sleep I could find out. But I can tell he's kind of hurt that it wasn't him in the dream. Jesus! What a baby. So I tell him about my sense-memory exercise in class, how I had to think of something good I'd done for somebody. . . .

You *told* the class that?

Sure, I say. I mean, why not?

He goes, you didn't tell them my name, did you?

Of course not, I go. Like it would mean anything to them anyway. Dean the Famous Bond Salesman.

Dean keeps saying over and over that he still can't believe that I told them. But I think secretly he's really flattered, you know?

Finally he asks me if I want to go to dinner and I say yeah, definitely, and he asks if I have any preference and I say Mexican, I don't know, I just suddenly have this craving for hot salsa and margaritas. Love that spicy food. Must be my southern blood, did I mention my mom's from Georgia? Anyway Dean says cool, he knows a place.

Are you sure that's okay? I go. I'm like suddenly thinking maybe he had some big plan that I spoiled. The last time I went out on an actual date this guy sent a limo around and we ate at Le Bernardin and he was all upset that all I wanted was a salad because he'd gone to all this trouble and I guess he had these visions of us feeding each other oysters and snails and lusting across the meat like Albert Finney and that chick in *Tom Jones,* but I felt like I'd done my bit spending about five hours on makeup and borrowing an Alaïa evening dress from Didi and emerald earrings from Jeannie. Granted, a salad's not very sexy but it's results that count, right? And any girl who gets invited out with any regularity and scarfs the paté and the tournedos and the mousse is eventually going to kill the goose that laid the golden egg, you know? Sure, there are fetishists who write letters to *Penthouse* about lusting after the fat girls, but let's face it . . . I mean, Alaïa doesn't make those sexy dresses in size fourteen. Which I've gotta say is Francesca's problem. That girl loves eating the way I love . . . well, let's just say the way Didi loves blow. We're talking addiction. It's sort of funny that they're friends, now that I think about it. Didi hasn't eaten in about eight months and Francesca never stops. Being in a restaurant with those two is a really weird experience. Didi jumping up to go to the Ladies every three minutes and Francesca screaming at the waitress to bring more bread. And butter. Luckily it doesn't happen too often since Didi can never get it together to show up anywhere.

Anyway, I'm talking about dinner plans, right? and I'm suddenly worried that Dean had some big romantic idea that I'd just blown, but he says Mex is fine, dress casual and he'll come by at eight-thirty.

Jeannie comes home a few minutes later. She throws herself down on the bed and says, God, I can't wait to get married so I can quit working and lie around the house all day.

Jeannie is engaged to this guy Frank Salton who's a tennis pro on Hilton Head. She flies down to see him every weekend, which is the main reason she has to have a job — that and a few other bad habits—since the allowance her parents give her only covers the rent plus one or two outfits a week. I was going to mention food but Jeannie doesn't really eat. They're supposed to get married this fall. I don't know. Frank's a decent guy—I know, because I introduced him to Jeannie. Actually that's kind of a problem. I went out with him before Jeannie. For about five minutes. But still. Anyway, she could definitely do better. Frank's got a decent body, but he's no brain surgeon. One time he broke his index finger and he couldn't read for six weeks, right? Had to skip the Sunday funnies till his pointer got better. Plus Jeannie is used to a lot of money and Frank's never going to make a ton of it. Not to be a snob. I don't think it's a reason not to get married, but it's kind of stupid, if you ask me, to pretend that these things don't make a difference.

Don't you ever just want somebody to take care of you? Jeannie says.

I go, I miss having a maid, if that's what you mean.

You know what I mean, she goes.

I'd get bored, I say. Having the same guy around all the time.

Not me, Jeannie says. I can't wait. I'm going to sit around and watch the soaps, eat bonbons, cook dinner, the whole thing.

I'm like, since when did you ever cook anything?

I can learn, she says.

You'd better, I go. On Frank's salary I don't think you're going to be able to afford help.

She goes, fuck you, Alison.

Hey, I go, I'm just being realistic.

I mean, really. I'm trying to tell her what life is really like. Wake up and smell the espresso, babe.

So Dean comes by and picks me up, looking good, casual and sexy in chinos and a cotton sweater. Even though she's not going out, Jeannie brushes her hair and touches up her eyes before he comes over. She gives him the eye and I can tell what she's thinking. It kills her that I went out with Frank, and she develops these weird physical crushes on any guy I go out with but I doubt she even realizes it. I think she'd like to sleep with all my boyfriends. Partly it's like a revenge fantasy, but also its because she loves me and looks up to me and sympathizes totally with me, you know, and automatically likes a guy if he's passed my selection process. Reminds me of my sister Carol, who never liked the clothes she bought for herself and only wanted to wear stuff from my closet. I guess it's a compliment. With Jeannie, it's kind of like, we share sweaters and shoes and dresses so why not men? At least, I sometimes think that's what's going on in her head when she starts flirting with my guys, though probably not consciously. It's sort of a great idea, sharing a lover with someone you love. But it's too weird, really.

Did I mention about Jeannie and Alex, my old boyfriend? Somewhere in Jeannie's mind there's this doubt about marriage and domestic bliss with Frank, this little cloud floating around—it's like, picture a perfectly clear sky and that's probably a pretty good picture of Jeannie's mind—I love her but I definitely wouldn't let her take my law boards for me. Anyway there's this little thing she has going over the phone with Alex, he calls up for me but sometimes she picks up or else I'm not home and they've developed this incredible flirtation where they're talking about sex and teasing each other and they've never even met. I told you about Jeannie and my boyfriends. In a way I'm kind of irritated but in another way I'm like, great, I hope Jeannie sleeps with Alex because if she does she'll have a hard time settling for the notion of a lifetime of sleeping with Frank, who is not exactly Valentino in bed. I think it would be good for her, and anyway, this marriage idea is kind of bogus. . . .

* * *

So Dean and I are in this frantic place on Second Avenue packed with well-groomed gringos getting sloppy on margaritas.

Popular place, I go.

Dean says, these people are all bankers trying to improve the balance of payments with Mexico and prevent default. That's the only way I can think of, he goes, to explain the popularity of Third World food on the Upper East Side.

Most of them look like they could use some spice, I say. Not that Dean is exactly the hairy barbarian himself. I mean, it seems like his idea of wild is argyle socks. But it's okay, I like straight guys, I'd never go out with anybody who's as irresponsible as me. Most of the guys I know have really high-powered jobs and make up for lost time when they're not in the office. The Berserk After Work Club. I seem to attract them in a big way, all these boys in Paul Stuart suits with six-figure salaries and hellfire on a dimmer switch in their eyes.

The waiter knows Dean and he keeps bringing us free maragaritas so I get really blasted. Not blasted exactly. I just get really horny. Story of my life, right? I mean, who needs tequila? But then I remember my little problem, which makes me a mondo unhappy unit.

Dean's like, you want to come over? and I'm like, sure, yeah, but basically I'm still out of commission. He says that's okay, sex isn't the only thing he ever thinks about, and I'm like, well, I hope it's near the top of the list, anyway. He cracks up.

# STORY OF MY LIFE

So we get to Dean's house and the phone is ringing. I don't know why I say house, it's an apartment. It's like, living in New York never really seems normal, you keep thinking of the world as a place where people live in houses and drive cars to the 7-Eleven.

Somebody called Didi for you, Dean goes, handing me the phone.

Didi's just bought her stash for the night and she wants to come over. God, I don't know. A couple of lines would be nice, but I've got class in the morning, plus it's Dean's apartment and it's not really up to me. So I go, you don't really want this beautiful maniac friend of mine coming over here and wiggling her cute little tail all over the place and forcing nonprescription drugs up your nose, do you?

And he says, sounds terrible, ask her how soon she can get here, and I go, really, you don't mind? and he goes, why not? And I figure, well, I tried, right? but just to be safe I check my watch—it's a little after eleven—and I say to Dean, we definitely kick her out at one, right? If not sooner.

Absolutely, he says.

And suddenly Dean goes, wait a minute, this isn't Didi Spence, is it? Well, it turns out Dean knows Didi's cousin Phil. And of course he's heard stories. I don't think there's anybody in New York who hasn't heard about Didi.

Listen, I go, you better not start drooling all over Didi in front of me.

And he goes, Alison, I only have eyes for you.

I'm like, right, Dean. If you think I believe that I've got some swampland in Florida I'll sell you real cheap.

* * *

Didi shows up a little after midnight.

By this time I'm chewing my fingernails off thinking about getting a line, right? If she hadn't called at all that would've suited me just fine. We're watching Carson, I'm kind of giving Dean a backrub. It must be bimbo night. I can't believe some of the so-called actresses who are making a killing out there in videoland. You can see, when they get live on Johnny, these starlets without stage training, that they don't even know how to talk. Doing a TV series they can shoot five hundred takes while some dimwit walking talking inflatable doll who the producer slept with tries to learn how to say Gesundheit! Or they can just change the script and say, bless you! and the prompter gives the lines word by word offscreen and then the editor cuts away just before she starts to pick her nose. I'm sorry, but the stage is where real actors and actresses live and die. You can't fake it up there. We're talking truth in advertising. My teacher says acting is about truth, and I finally figured out what he means, you know what real acting is when you see this fake shit on television. I'm not saying I'd turn down a role in a movie or even a TV series. But there's a lot of bimbos making huge bucks. I can't stand watching Johnny pimp for NBC's latest sitcom, so we switch to Channel J to check out "Midnight Blue," that cable show that's all T and A and hand-held cameras and ads for escort services . . . which is like a blast of honesty and fresh air after this horrible network cosmetology.

So finally the buzzer rings in the middle of the nude talk show. Didi breezes in wearing the same clothes she had on before she went to bed this afternoon. Still, I can see that

Dean thinks she's all right. Any minute the saliva will start trickling down his chin. Sometimes I wonder why all my friends are good-looking. I must be an idiot.

Mirror, says Didi, before she's even inside the door.

I know your cousin Phil, Dean drools.

Didi ignores Dean and walks over to draw the living room curtains. Dean gets her a picture from the wall, a framed poster for a play called *Zoo Story,* sounds like something I could relate to. Didi sits down on the floor in front of the coffee table and dumps out a mound of blow.

I'm so mad at Whitney, Didi says, launching into a story about a friend of ours who's supposedly spreading rumors about Didi. I don't know why Whitney would want to spread rumors about Didi, the truth's kinky enough. Dean is a little stunned. This chick has just walked in and taken over his apartment, like an army commander or something. She chops and folds the stuff endlessly until I'm about ready to hit her over the head with the brass lamp. Dean rolls up a bill, probably just trying to be helpful, although I think he's a little impatient too. Didi doesn't even look at Dean's bill. I don't know, she is rude, but it's kind of like what do you call it, a parachuter who won't let anyone else pack his parachute. Didi's into the ritual and the equipment. It's what she does. When she's good and ready, she rolls her own bill, does a couple of monster lines—what Didi calls lines other people call grams—and then tortures us for a few more minutes holding the rolled bill in the air and waving it around while she bitches some more about Whitney. Finally the spoiled little brat lets us play with her toys and she looks around for the first time.

This your place? she says to Dean.

Dean looks up from the mirror and nods his head so hard I'm afraid he's going to break his neck.

You own or rent? Didi asks, lighting up a Merit.

Rent, Dean says.

The buzzer rings and Didi goes, that's probably Francesca. And I'm like, Didi, what's the deal here? and Didi goes relax. Dean goes to the door and comes back with Francesca and Jeannie. Naturally we hear Francesca's voice even before Dean gets the door open, and I'm sure his neighbors do too. And isn't it interesting that Jeannie's dressed to kill? A few hours ago she's all set to go to bed, and now she's in black cashmere and hose. Plus we should've bought stock in Chanel before she started in on her face tonight. Didi and me usually just wear leggings under a shirt or something, except I change mine every day, but Jeannie and Francesca wouldn't think of going out of the house without a thousand bucks worth of fabric on their backs. Jeannie has this expensive WASP look and Francesca's dressed as usual, sort of the expensive-flooze chic—sequins and cleavage—which actually does suit her. I mean, if you're pushing size 12 and headed for a D cup, you might as well go for it. She gives me a huge hug while she finishes this urgent story that she's right in the middle of, which has something to do with some rock singer.

Do a line, Didi demands. Everybody do a line. House rules.

Didi can't stand it, of course, that someone else has center stage when she's the one who brought the drugs. Plus it bugs her that Francesca doesn't do drugs—for someone like Didi, health, sanity and moderation are like a personal affront.

Jeannie doesn't have to be asked twice, she dives right in.

Francesca ignores her and says, I'm so upset, there's the ugliest picture of me in *Women's Wear* at Nan Kempner's party and I look so fat, the caption says, Francesca Green, also known as the Goodyear Blintz, wearing a waterproof canvas tent by L. L. Bean. I swear to God that's what it looks like in the picture. I've got to go on a diet. Even I'm grossed out by myself and I don't scare easy. No wonder I haven't been laid since boarding school. Not that there are any men out there worth breaking a sweat with. They're all jerks, basically. Present company excluded, Dean honey. Ooh, he's so cute isn't he? (She goes over and hugs Dean, gives him a big kiss. She just totally cracks me up.) Not my type though, she says. Too clean-cut. I like them mean and nasty-looking. I want guitar heroes and boys who were raised on the streets by wolves. Attila the Hun is my basic dream lover. Oh, God, did I tell you guys I met David Lee Roth the other night at Raoul's? That boy is to die for. . . .

Will you stop babbling and let somebody else talk for a change? Didi says. She's furiously chopping up more blow, after Jeannie did the last four lines. Jeannie's sitting demurely on the couch with her legs crossed and her hands folded on her knees in her finishing school manner, posing for Dean while she pretends to listen to Francesca. Sometimes I think the only good thing you can say about cocaine is that it affects Jeannie the exact opposite way it affects everyone else, she clams up for the whole night, lockjaw, so we don't have to listen to her flirt.

Meanwhile, Dean's like the cock of the walk, looking every which way. I think he likes having four young girls in his apartment, even if he doesn't quite know how to handle all this estrogen in the air. Looking over at him nodding and beaming at Francesca and then Didi makes me want to grab him and drag him off to the bedroom. He's got those swimming-pool eyes, you want to dive right in.

Did you hear about Kristin? Francesca says.

Didi shouts, boring, boring. New rule, she goes. No talking about boring subjects.

Francesca goes, so what shall we talk about? Your drug habit?

I don't have a drug habit, Didi says. I do drugs because I love them. Habits are boring routines.

We all kind of roll our eyes while Didi goes down on the mirror. Even my guy looks a little skeptical and he's only known Didi for an hour.

I'm certainly glad to hear that, Dean says. Otherwise I'm afraid I'd have to ask you to leave the premises immediately.

I know, says Didi when she comes up for air.

What? I go.

Truth or Dare, she says.

Oh, no, says Jeannie.

We can't subject Dean to Truth or Dare the first night, Francesca goes.

Didi goes, it's not the first night. Alison went down on him last night.

Thanks for reminding us of that, Didi. Jesus.

Dean's got instant sunburn. He's like, is there anything else that you all would like to know about me? I'd hate to think I was holding anything back.

Jeannie says, do you have a brother?

He shakes his head, then he says, what's Truth or Dare?

I don't know—I'm a little dubious. I mean, I did just meet him and Truth or Dare can get pretty heavy. Plus I want to be in bed in about twenty minutes. I check my watch—definitely no more than half an hour for sure.

Didi explains the rules. You've got to be into it, she says. Everybody has to swear at the beginning to tell the truth, because otherwise there's no point. When it's your turn you say either truth or dare. If you say truth, you have to answer whatever question you're asked. And if you say dare, then you have to do whatever somebody dares you to do.

Whatever? says Dean, with this big grin on his face.

Within reason, Didi says. No physical violence and no sexual contact, but anything else.

Didi just likes this game because she's an exhibitionist, Francesca says. She can't wait to take her clothes off.

Shut up, says Didi. Now, everybody has to do two big lines to start out. Then I'll go first.

Didi starts with me, which figures.

Alison, she goes. Were you physically attracted to Dean when you first saw him?

For Didi that's pretty tame. I kind of wish she hadn't asked me, but I have to answer no. Then I look over at Dean and add, not at first, but Didi waves her arm and says, no, no explanations, no excuses. I want a simple yes-or-no answer.

Then it's my turn. So I turn to Jeannie and say truth or dare and she says truth, so I say, are you physically attracted to Dean? Partly because I want her to admit it and partly because it will cheer Dean up to hear it.

Jeannie nods. Dean smiles. So now it's Jeannie's turn. Jeannie asks Francesca if she ever slept with this hunky guy who worked the stables at this fairground in Harrisburg and

Francesca says they actually did go to this motel room and everything but this guy brought a bottle of tequila and he got so drunk he passed out.

And Jeannie mentioning Harrisburg reminds me of this big trip we all made out there to look at Dangerous Dan, the whole nuclear family, actually driving down the interstate in a station wagon like normal people. Dad had come back for a trial reconciliation and I desperately wanted this horse Dangerous Dan so Dad decides we'll make a family expedition out of it. Me and Rebecca and Carol squabbling in the back and playing license plate games, Mom and Dad up front being seriously polite to each other. Wow, that's as weird as it gets—the American family.

Anyway, after that station break it's back to Truth or Dare, which so far is pretty harmless. I can see Didi getting restless already, chopping more lines. Francesca says, Didi, truth or dare, and then when Didi looks up Cesca says, and don't say dare, because I have no desire to see your body.

Okay, Didi goes, truth.

And Francesca asks her if she was the one who started this rumor about Francesca which is too complicated and boring to explain, but Didi says no, it wasn't her, and Francesca says she's glad, and then Didi looks at me and I'm like, uh-oh, I can see trouble coming here, and she goes, Alison, on a scale of one to ten, how would you rate Skip Pendleton in bed?

Didi is such a bitch sometimes. She really knows how to cause trouble, which is probably the whole point of this game, to hit where it hurts, but I know Dean is pretty sensitive about the whole Skip Pendleton thing. But what can I do? I'd give him an eight, I go. Eight, eight and a half.

Dean's wincing but hey, once you start lying it's hard to stop and I just plain refuse. If I thought Skip was a ten I would've said so, but that way if I told Dean he was a ten someday, or that I loved him, he'd know I was telling the truth.

So it's my turn and I go to Dean, truth or dare, and he takes truth so I go, did that bother you just now, about Skip Pendleton?

He thinks about it for a little while, so of course I already know what his answer is and finally he goes, yeah, a little.

So I go over and give him a big hug and say, poor baby.

And he says, not really.

And Didi screams, stop it, no mushy stuff, not playing the game.

So then it's Dean's turn and I see him looking around and suddenly it's like clear as fucking Evian water that he's checking out Didi's body and wondering if she really would strip down. And I'm like, well, I suppose I can't really blame him, and I figure I've hurt his feelings so what the hell, you know, and so I say, go ahead, Dean, ask Didi.

And Dean goes, Didi, truth or dare and Didi looks around with this real world-weary look, like a movie star being asked to sign one more autograph, because usually we play this game with a whole bunch of guys and they're constantly daring Didi to take off her clothes. And she's like, okay, dare.

Dean looks over at me and I shrug and tell him to go ahead. And he scrunches up his forehead and squints at me, like—really? And I think, the thing that's really going to piss me off is if he wants to see Didi naked but he's too much of a wimp to ask. If there's one thing I hate it's dishonesty. Drives me crazy. I hate liars and hypocrites. And I'm not too big on wimps, either.

Take off your clothes, Dean says.

Not this again, Francesca says. I think I'm going to puke.

Is that all? Didi says. You could at least be a little more imaginative.

And Dean says, that's all, which makes the whole thing all right for me, the fact that he doesn't let her push him around. I mean, I'm a little bugged, sure, but I'm glad he's not a wimp.

So Didi does one more line and then stands up and says where? and Dean shrugs and goes, right there is fine. So Didi pulls off her shirt and of course she's not wearing a bra, and I hate to say it but she has these perfectly shaped breasts and then she takes off her jeans which don't have any panties underneath and I'm looking at Dean who is definitely impressed, which isn't surprising. He looks a little embarrassed, but he's not looking away either.

Didi goes, ta-da, like she's real bored, but she wouldn't do it if she weren't getting off.

Give me a break, for Christ's sake, says Francesca.

Didi shakes her hips, pirouettes like a runway model and then goes, okay?

Dean nods, very serious, like someone's asked him if he's ready to leave the art museum.

So Didi puts her clothes back on and at least that's over with for the night.

Francesca goes, it's been fun, boys and girls, but I've got to work in the morning.

Me too, says Jeannie. I'd almost forgotten she's still here.

And I look at my watch and it's two-thirty and I say, ditto, I've got class, I've got to get some sleep.

Nobody's leaving, Didi screams. No fair. I've been sharing all my blow with you and now you're just going to leave me all alone when I'm a shivering wreck. No fair. You all have to stay for a while and help me come down.

Actually, come to think of it, I couldn't sleep now anyway. I'm kind of a shivering wreck myself. I've been pacing the room for the last ten minutes and sucking down cigarettes and my heart's thumping like a fat girl on a trampoline.

Didi dumps out some more blow. Two more lines for everybody and then we'll take some Valium, she says.

I don't want the lines, I go. I just want the Valium.

No way, she says. Two lines for everybody. Including Francesca. House rules. And one more round of Truth or Dare. My turn. I earned my question.

Francesca goes, it's your party and you'll whine if you want to, and we all crack up.

Didi hoovers a monster line and then passes the mirror. She says, my turn to ask, shut up everybody. She turns back to Dean. He takes truth. She goes, two-part question. On a scale of one to ten, how would you rate my body and how would you rate Alison's body?

I'm like, you bitch, Didi. I'm going to kill you one of these days.

Dean looks like he's hoping for nuclear war to break out in the next thirty seconds.

Truth, says Didi.

Can I take the dare? Dean asks.

Nobody wants to see your body, Didi says.

I wouldn't mind, says Francesca, and Jeannie, who's trying to get her nostrils to work, says, me neither.

Rules are rules, says Didi. Truth.

Dean looks back and forth between us and finally he says, I'd give you both a nine and a half.

Give me a break, says Francesca.

Diplomacy is strictly against the rules, Didi goes.

So then the phone rings.

Dean jumps for it. Someone named Rebecca, he goes, wants to talk to either Alison or Didi.

I'm like, now what?

Rebecca says, Alison, is that you? Listen, you gotta help me. I need to get five hundred dollars quick or I'm going to get sliced up with a knife.

# 5
# CARE OF THE SOCIAL FABRIC

So we're lying in Dean's bed, finally coming down on the Valium, but still grinding our teeth because they were only the five-milligram and Didi only gave us two. Semishivering. It's been one of those nights. I'm just beginning to really hate myself because I know I'm not going to be in any shape to go to class tomorrow and Dean's got to be at work in a couple of hours, poor guy, but then I think, well, we were saving Rebecca's life, right? It was a special occasion. It's not like I was just partying till dawn.

Suddenly Dean goes, are you mad at me?

And I go, about what?

And he goes, about daring Didi to take her clothes off.

I don't know, I say. Should I be? Do you want to sleep with her?

No, he says, I don't.

Truth, I say.

Really, he says. I don't. She's too weird. I can't imagine it. She's a harpy disguised as an angel.

That's exactly how he talks, I kid you not.

But you liked her body, I go.

Well, yeah, he says, I did. Can you understand that?

I'm not mad at you for that, I tell him. But I am mad at you for lying.

When did I lie? he says. He sits up in bed and looks at me with these big puppy eyes. He *is* cute. I wish I didn't have this stupid infection—I'm almost cooled out enough to have sex.

You lied, I say, when you rated my body the same as Didi's.

That wasn't a lie, he says, but he turns his eyes away from me when he says it.

Come on, I go, can you honestly sit there and tell me you think my body's as good as hers?

Sure, he whines. Jesus, you've got an incredible body.

I say, but not as incredible as hers.

Better, he goes.

I'm like, now I'm really getting pissed.

What did I do? he goes.

You're not being honest, I say. You're thinking one thing and saying another.

Not necessarily, he says.

Yes necessarily, I tell him.

In my experience this is one big problem with older

guys, they start to lose their spontaneity in their thirties, start saying what they think they're supposed to say instead of what they feel, sort of like hardening of the arteries. Like, we're all pretty much raving maniacs as kids, but then some of us get all conventional. Not me, that's why I know I'm going to be a great actress some day, I'm totally in touch with my child.

Alison, Dean goes, in this older-man kind of tone, let's just imagine that a guy had just met a girl he really likes. This is strictly hypothetical, right? But let's say that shortly after he meets her, and before he even knows her very well, somebody asks him, in her presence, who's prettier, her or, for instance, his former girlfriend. Right? Now, don't you think he'd be a real pig if he said, in front of this nice new girl, that his old girlfriend made her, his new female friend, look like Lassie?

I'm like, you think I look like Lassie, huh?

Dean's like, Alison! That's just an example. A deliberately extreme one.

So your old squeeze is prettier than me, is that it? I say.

He says, I'm just saying that even if I were lying, which I wasn't—truth isn't always an unalloyed virtue.

I go, a what?

Unalloyed, he says. That means pure.

And I'm like, no wonder I don't know it.

And he says, there are times when it's better to spare people's feelings, keep the social fabric intact.

And I'm like, the social fabric? What the hell is that? I go, is that like dacron polyester or something?

I mean really, he believes this shit?

Actually, it's more like silk, he says. It's a delicate thing.

It's like nonexistent is what I'm saying, I go. We're all just pieces of lint if you ask me.

That's very clever, Alison, he goes, hauling out the grown-up moan again. Look, he says, I'm just saying there's a reason for manners. The unvarnished truth isn't always what we need to hear. Diplomacy is what separates us from the animals.

I totally disagree, I say. I've grown up around liars and cheaters and I don't think there's any excuse for not telling the truth. I want to be able to trust you, but if I don't think you respect the truth, you know, then I'll just hit the road. You've got a nice vocabulary but I'm like, I insist on honesty. You should be able to tell me whatever you're feeling. If you think Didi has a better body than me you should say so. I can take it.

Dean says, and what if I do want to sleep with her?

Then you should, I go. Don't hold off on my account.

You don't mean that, he goes.

I do too, I say. I hope you don't want to. But if you do, you should.

There are some things you feel that you would never act on, Dean says, and there are some things you feel that you'd never want to say. Do you think I should sleep with everyone I'm attracted to? How far does this honesty go?

If I want to do something, I do it, I say. If I feel something I say it. Otherwise you're a hypocrite.

Have you ever wanted to kill someone, Alison? he says.

A lot of people, I go.

But you didn't, right? You can't act out all your impulses.

And I'm like, some of them I wish I had.

Dean lies back down and I can't even hear him breathing. After a few minutes I begin to feel bad about giving him such a hard time, especially since he was so great about helping Rebecca, so I roll over and curl up in his shoulder, then I kiss his ear and finally he leans over and kisses me on the mouth and one things leads to another and pretty soon we're in the same spot we were in the night before. I mean, I am one horny unit, but then the phone rings—for some reason Dean forgot to unplug it or turn on the machine, I don't know, maybe his friends don't call at all hours. I would've ignored it, but he picks it up and of course it's Rebecca. I look at the clock and it's 5:15.

What are you doing? Rebecca says.

I'm drinking tea with Princess Di, I go.

We're over at Didi's partying, she goes.

And I'm like, imagine my surprise.

She says, I wanted to ask you something but now I can't remember what it was.

I can hear Didi screaming something in the background.

So what's happening with you? says Rebecca.

Finally I get rid of Rebecca and apologize to Dean. He says it's okay and maybe we should get some sleep. What a wacky idea. I tell him he better unplug the phone. Becca will call back in five minutes once she remembers what she wanted to ask me. Probably she'll want to know the name of some kid who lived next door to us fifteen years ago or something like that. Or else she'll call up from the police station or the airport or from the apartment of some drug dealer who wants to kill her, like the first time she called tonight about three hours ago—it seems like weeks.

She's like, I need to get five hundred dollars quick or I'm going to get sliced up with a knife.

And I'm like, whoa, is this a joke, or what? Nothing would surprise me coming from Rebecca, but still, this sounds a little radical.

Alison, she goes, I'm not kidding.

So I get the address and then Dean and Didi and me hop in a cab. Francesca gives us seventy dollars and Jeannie has forty. Dean gets two hundred out of his cash machine and Didi gets a hundred, which is all she has left, and then we go and wake up our friend Whitney and hit her bank. Feels kind of like old times, scraping up cash to visit Emile—except I'm really scared for Rebecca and I'm thinking about some guy cutting her up while we're waiting for the damn computer at Chase Manhattan. *¡No más!*

So we fly up to Morningside Heights and Dean tells the cab driver the faster the trip the bigger the tip and finally we get up to this street of falling-down brownstones and find the right number. Dean says he's going to go up alone and I say, no way, I'm coming too, and Didi says she doesn't want to sit outside by herself. Dean's so cool, I mean, he doesn't even know Rebecca and he might get killed, I'm real grateful and I say later on I'll show him just how grateful I can be, but right now I tell him she's my sister and I'm coming up too. Then we hassle with the taxi driver, who naturally doesn't want to hang around. In this neighborhood, he says, you get bullets through the windows. Dean gives him some huge tip and asks him to circle the block four or five times and watch for us. Then we go up.

The front door is open already, busted on the hinges. The front hall is full of beer cans and crack vials. As we walk up the stairs I can hear the vials popping under our feet, snap crackle pop, breaking like little promises. We knock at the third-floor landing. After a while some voice goes yeah and I go, it's Rebecca's sister. The guy goes, you got the money? and I say yeah and then the door opens on a chain and these eyes look out, these dark, pinwheel eyes, and the guy goes, who are all these people? So we have this big debate at the door and he says he wants to see the money and I say I want to see Rebecca and finally she comes to the door and says, let them in for Christ's sake, Mannie.

So the guy opens the door and lets us in. He's holding this knife, just kind of pointing it at us in general, but it doesn't look like he'd really know what to do with it if it came down to that. He looks scared and sheepish. He's maybe my age, small and skinny, about the size of Prince, with that same ridiculous little mustache, not bad-looking actually.

Put the stupid knife away, for Christ's sake, Rebecca says. They've brought the money. She's drinking a beer, wearing a red Danskin top, these X-rated shorts and Reeboks. She looks like she's all set for aerobics, her hair up in a ponytail. I don't know, I expected her to be tied up or something. It's kind of an anticlimax.

Dean gives the money to Becca and she gives it to this guy Mannie and he shoves it in his pocket and then folds up the knife. I don't know why but I feel sorry for him. He looks so scared and lonely on the opposite side of the room from the rest of us.

We had an agreement, he says. She owed me that money fair and square. She was here last week. I trusted her for the bread.

You told me I didn't have to pay.

That was different, Mannie says.

Different than what? Rebecca says. You just thought you'd get to fuck me.

Mannie looks down at the floor. We had an agreement, he whines.

Becca says, let's get out of here, and then in the same breath she goes, if you guys have another hundred we can get an eighth for the road. I've got one fifty.

Rebecca is totally in character.

That's a good idea, says Didi.

So I don't know, it was hard to get the story out of Rebecca. She said she met this guy last week at the China Club and he gave her a quarter ounce and his phone number, so when she goes up there to get some more he demands five hundred dollars. I don't know what to believe, I really don't. Little Mannie is apologizing like crazy as we're leaving. Then he asks Becca to please call him, almost crying. I don't know what the attraction is—drug dealers, investment bankers, she turns them all into blubbering idiots.

Did anybody else think he looked kind of like Prince? I go when we're riding back downtown.

I thought he looked like Jesus, Rebecca said.

Of course I sleep through my classes. When I finally open my eyes long enough to focus on anything it's almost two, and I vaguely remember Dean getting up and leaving for his office. I grab the channel-changer by the bed and flip on "All

My Children." When I finally get my act together and go home it's three-thirty.

I'm about to take a shower because I smell like an all-nighter, then I think I'll take a bath so I can have a faucet orgasm. After all, I didn't get any last night. A faucet orgasm is pretty much the same principle as a bidet orgasm except upside-down. When we were growing up we had bidets in all the bathrooms and when I was about ten I accidentally discovered one of the things they were good for. After that I used to spend hours on the damn thing. This dump we rent doesn't have a bidet so I have to get in the tub and slide up toward the front, running my legs up the wall on either side of the faucet. Turn on the warm water and smile. Actually, you've got to get the water temperature just right first or you could really be in for a nasty shock. I've made that mistake a few times. This time I get it just right and I come three times before I get around to actually taking a bath.

After toweling off and dosing up with some baby powder, I flop down on the bed and next thing I know I'm asleep again.

I love to sleep. My dreams are so good, sometimes when I wake up in the middle of a really good one I go right back to sleep to see if I can get back into it. Once in a while it works. I don't think most people appreciate dreams enough. They don't remember or else they try to interpret them, you know, like they aren't any good unless they have some application in real life. I think you should just take them for what they are. I mean, I love sex dreams but if I believed this psych course I took in college, then all dreams are sex dreams, which is ridiculous. Believe me, I know sex when I dream it, and I'm about the last person in the world to underestimate it, but who represses their sexual desires anymore? Nobody I know. Well, maybe we sometimes resist the urge to jump on top of some guy in the elevator or on the sidewalk. But we probably give him our phone number for later that night.

Really, though, sex isn't the only thing in life or in dreams—I can hear some of my friends who are like, unbelievable, Alison admitting sex isn't everything. I used to be a bit of a slut. But anyway, about dreams, there are dreams about flying and swimming and eating and things that you can't even describe, which is what's so great about dreaming. I hate these people who try to make everything fit some scheme. Professors and shrinks. Francesca's parents really wanted her to go to a shrink just in case there was anything wrong with her, in case they screwed up somehow, so they can feel better about it in advance of even knowing about it and feeling guilty, so she goes twice a week and sometimes when she's real bored she'll dish out some really bogus crap about her childhood or her dreams and take the shrink for a horrible ride into fantasyland. Like, gee, I had this dream where my father was smoking a big cigar and stroking my inner thigh, gosh, what do you suppose it means?

When Jeannie comes home from work and wakes me up I've been dreaming this dream where the bunch of us from last night are all sitting around Dean's apartment playing Truth or Dare. My acting coach is there too. But it turns out that Dean's apartment is actually on the stage of the Public Theater and there's this huge audience out there watching us play Truth or Dare. TRUTH OR DARE is spelled out in flashing light bulbs over the stage and my acting coach has a microphone, he's moderating the whole thing, like a TV game-show host. . . .

## STORY OF MY LIFE

Jeannie's in a real pissy mood and gets right on the phone to her fiancé, so I watch "Wheel of Fortune" in the bedroom. When she's finally finished discussing world literature and nuclear disarmament with Frank she hangs up and calls the deli to order some Diet Coke and a large bag of barbecue potato chips and a pack of Merit Ultra Lights. I stick my head out the door because I want to order a pack of cigarettes myself but she's already hung up. She picks up a copy of *Cosmo* and shuffles back and forth through the pages like they're playing cards that she's trying to seriously injure in the process. I think she's mad at me.

So I go back in the bedroom and call Dean and get his machine. I leave a message that's cheerier than I feel and then I call Carol, my little sister, but there's no answer. And then, like an optimist, I call Dad but of course there's no answer there. I'm such a sucker—every time I dial him I can't help getting this little tingle of hope. It's a miracle if I can even find him, but I sort of fantasize that he'll pick up the phone some day and say, is that you, Alison? I love you, honey, and I'm really sorry about the last fifteen years or so, I don't know what came over me but I'm better now and I'm so sorry. . . .

Jeannie picks up the phone in the other room while it's still ringing and says, oh, excuse me, really bitchy, and then slams it down.

There's no answer, anyway. After I hang up Jeannie calls up Alex, my old squeeze, it doesn't take long to figure this out because she keeps repeating his name and laughing real loud so I'll know who it is and what a great time she's having talking to my old boyfriend.

A few minutes after she hangs up Jeannie finally comes

in and sits down on the bed, viciously crunching away on her potato chips. I hate to see her expending so much energy on getting me to notice that she's not a happy unit, so I say to her, are you mad at me? I remember as I say it that Dean asked me that same question about twelve hours ago.

Who, me? she says, with a big fake look of horror. Mad at you? Why should I be mad at you? Just because you accused me in public of wanting to sleep with your boyfriend, is that any reason for me to be mad at you?

I bet Jeannie's been rehearsing those lines all day.

Well, don't you? I say.

No, I don't. For one thing I don't find him irresistible, no offense, and for another thing he's your boyfriend and some of us are loyal to our friends.

Well, I'm sorry, I say, I guess I was wrong. And I feel kind of guilty when she says loyal to our friends because I have been awfully hard on her lately, I don't know what's wrong with me, I love Jeannie.

And Jeannie goes what? The infallible Alison? Wrong? Impossible. God, I hate George Michael, she says, watching his video on MTV.

I could say, well, that's what channel-changers are for, babe, but instead I say, I don't trust men whose last names sound like first names.

Jeannie says, I don't trust men, period.

Well, at least it's not just me she's mad at. I ask her if there's trouble with Frank and she launches into this thing about how Frank suddenly told her he can't come up for the weekend which was the plan because supposedly the other tennis pro suddenly came down with a sick grandmother and he has to cover all weekend. I'm like, sick grandmother? give me a break. Or maybe the dog ate his homework, right? And not only can't he come up but he'll also be too busy to see her, she really wouldn't have a good time down there blah blah blah and Jeannie, not real surprisingly, isn't sure she believes him. She thinks something's rotten on the island of Hilton Head.

So I do my bit. Come on, I tell her, he's probably telling the truth, she should trust him, she's going to marry the guy and trust is the basis of marriage and she can always wake up really early Saturday morning and call him if she thinks he might be slipping around, see if he's actually home and if he sounds guilty. Or if she really wants to do a serious bedcheck she could fly down unannounced.

She says that's a great idea, it cheers her up, she decides to go for it and surprise dear old Frankie. She hugs me and I hug her back. She calls up the airline and reserves for an 8:00 A.M. flight.

You going to be able to wake up for that one? I say.

I may just stay awake, she says. God, this is great, I should be able to get to his apartment by ten, which is plenty of time.

She's dying to catch Frank in the act. It's nice to see her smiling again, but what a smile, all teeth and gums, like a piranha. She calls the limo service and books a car to pick her up Saturday morning.

Alison, she goes, you're a genius.

All this boyfriend stuff makes me think of Dean. I call him and get the machine again. This time I leave a really neutral message asking him to call me when he gets in, very demure and ladylike. That's me.

Jeannie and I talk for a while about what dickheads men are and then we watch some dumb TV movie, as if there's any other kind, I couldn't begin to tell you what it's all about because my concentration is shot, I'm thinking about Dean, wondering where he is. It's after nine so he's probably at dinner somewhere. I remember he said he likes Indochine so I call up there but they say he's not there. I try to remember the name of his old girlfriend. I could just call and hang up if he answered. . . .

Then I think, what am I doing? This isn't me. This is somebody else. I've been in lust for three days and I'm acting like a jealous wife. I can't believe this. I mean, I love men in general, I'm a huge fan, but I'm never going to make a fool out of myself over any one in particular. Not after Alex. So what's my problem? Maybe I'm just going to have to give up on old Dean right now. I don't need this emotional stuff in my life. I've got my acting, I've got my sanity.

Then I remember he said he'd call. So I'll probably hear from him, right? It reminds me of that song, if the phone doesn't ring you'll know that it's me. I try to concentrate on the so-called movie, Richard fucking Chamberlain looking soulful in his beard as per usual, exotic locations, I can't even begin to figure out what's going on, goddamn him it's almost eleven o'clock. I can imagine Dean looking like Richard Chamberlain in about twenty years. . . .

Settle down, says Jeannie after I accidentally spill the ashtray all over the covers. So I tell her about why I'm so bugged and she tells me don't worry, he's probably got some business dinner or something.

* * *

At two-thirty Jeannie's sound asleep and I'm still staring at the TV set, wide awake with no help from artificial stimulants and no hope of artificial depressants. I absolutely cannot miss class again tomorrow. I get up and look in the medicine cabinet. Midol, Tylenol, a lot of other useless shit. I find a couple of Unisoms inside an old Halcyon prescription and take one. Back in bed, I think about calling. Should I act mad? Just a little hurt, maybe? Should I be cool and not even call? That's what I should do. It would be uncool to call. But right now I can't even sleep.

The phone rings and I practically break Jeannie's nose grabbing for it. Jeannie goes, mumble mumble growl snore.

Rebecca says, hi, sis.

What? I go.

I just remembered what I wanted to ask you, she says.

Where are you, I ask.

She says, me and Didi are at some guy's apartment.

So what did you want to ask? I say.

She goes, you remember that nursery rhyme we used to say in school, I'm trying to remember the words.

Rebecca, I go, there were only about five hundred nursery rhymes we used to say.

This is the one about Miss Mary Mack, she says.

Oh, right, I go. Miss Mary Mack Mack Mack all dressed in black black black with silver buttons buttons buttons all down her back back back . . .

Yeah, she says, that's it. How does the rest of it go?

I'm like, that's all I can remember right now.

Are you sure? she says.

I don't know, I say, not right now.

I hate to admit it, but it's actually bugging me that I can't remember the rest.

Try and remember, she says, I'll call back later.

And I'm like, no way, don't call back, I've got class tomorrow. How's Didi? I ask.

She's out of her mind, Rebecca says. Completely insane.

I go, so what else is new?

She's got a drug problem, says Rebecca.

Which is pretty funny coming from her. Didi says the same thing about Rebecca. People who are really fucked up love having somebody who they can think is a little farther out on the limb.

After I hang up I call Dean and get the machine with his boring message.

Goddamnit, now I'm really mad. Still, if I show I'm mad he might just get really turned off and think, what right does she have, I've only known her three days. What I really am is mad at myself. He doesn't owe me shit, it's not like we have a relationship. God, I hate that word, it's the death sentence for fun. Like, now we're having a relationship, how should we act? It's almost as bad as marriage. Once you say those words you get rules and definitions and you start losing track of your feelings and then they die. It's like, as soon as *Time* magazine comes up with a name for something you know it's already not happening anymore, it's already over.

Why the hell should sex get all mixed up with emotions? Forget it. It's just skin rubbing against skin in the night. It's just contact. There's no need to get all soppy about it afterwards. Fuck Dean. Who needs it?

I mean, why does stimulation always lead to aggravation? Explain that to me, will you please?

I must've fallen asleep at some point because eventually I wake up. Jeannie's at work. I'm on my way out the door to class when I get a call from this guy Brad I met in L.A. He's in New York and wonders what I'm doing tonight. He's pretty cute, I remember. I think.

I don't know, I go, make me an offer.

He says how about theater and dinner, and I figure why not, it's Friday noon and I'm not the kind of girl who spends Friday night waiting by the phone, I'm sorry but there's no way, not for all the Deans in the world. So I say sure and he says he'll pick me up at seven-thirty.

So it's seven-fifteen and I'm trying to figure out what to wear, I have absolutely no clothes, when dickhead, my true love, calls. Just perfect.

Hey, he goes, it's Dean.

Could you spell that for me? I say.

Sorry I didn't get back to you last night, he says. I had a business dinner that ran late.

Yeah, I go. I put a lot of spin on it.

What are you doing tonight? he goes.

I'm like, I've got a date.

He sounds pretty surprised. I tell him I'm a popular girl, he should book in advance. He asks about tomorrow and I say it's possible, and then he says he'll let me go. He sounds so sad I'm practically crying by the time I hang up. I think about calling and canceling Brad, but it's too late, in fact the buzzer rings and I'm still half naked and I haven't even started my makeup.

We go to this play, *Liaisons Dangereuses,* it's all about French people cooking up these sexual conspiracies, it's not the sex they like so much as the planning and scheming to corrupt virgins and housewives, it's all mental, but the worst guy of them all, the hero of the play, falls in love in spite of himself with this woman he's trying to seduce on a bet and it really fucks him up.

Hey, tell me about it.

The play's fine, I enjoy it, but it turns out Brad is a totally different guy than the guy I was thinking of, he's not so cute and afterwards he has to drag us backstage to say hello to one of the actresses who's this great friend of his, and after we finally get back there and wait for all the other great friends of hers to have their little chat Brad goes, hi, Bradley Stone, and when that doesn't bring the house down—I mean, she looks at him like he's Chinese or something—he goes, we met at Morton's with Carol and Rick, and it's obvious she doesn't have a clue who he is. And then he has to drag me into this mess just to spread the embarrassment around and he goes, this is Alison Poole, she's an actress herself. . . .

I don't even want to talk about it. I wanted to just disappear, I would have gladly melted into a puddle right there at her feet like the wicked witch in *The Wizard of Oz,* leaving nothing behind but some goo and this sapphire brooch I borrowed from Jeannie that I have to hold on to because it keeps coming undone. I don't know, he meant well, but there comes a point sometimes when you know you're in dating hell, when you've just got to grit your teeth and get through it, and I knew this was going to be one of those nights. I wasn't into it anyway, I kept thinking about Dean, but I thought I owed it to Brad to make the effort to act pleasant.

Then we go to the Four Seasons where Brad makes a big stink about getting a fountainside table, and he keeps repeating his name like it's a household word. Dinner lasts for three or four decades, I don't know, Brad's basically telling me all about how the entertainment industry would grind to a halt if anything happened to him, God forbid. That's sort of the moral of every story. This guy's a legend in his own mind.

Plus I freak out when I feel on my lapel for the sapphire brooch and it's not there, but amazingly it turns up under the table, the fastener thing that holds the pin part of it is really loose, I'm like—gasp, the thing is only worth ten years' rent, so I just hold it in my hand and squeeze hard when I think I'm going to fall asleep from boredom.

Finally he pays the check and wants to go to Nell's and I tell him I've got to be up early which is not necessarily a lie since I'll probably have to shake Jeannie awake at dawn to get her flight, she sleeps like a corpse.

Anyway, Brad gets all pissed off. Just one drink, he goes.

And I'm like, Jesus, I've heard that line before but I don't say it, I just smile demurely and say it's way past my bedtime.

He just happens to pick this moment to tell me he has tickets to the U2 concert at the Meadowlands tomorrow night. And I go, I still have to head home.

At the door of my apartment it's thanks for everything,

Brad. When he realizes I'm not going to invite him up, he goes, I think it's pretty rude after I've taken you to the theater and a pretty spectacular dinner to just . . .

To just what? I say after this long pause. He stopped when he realized what he was about to say. I go, do you mean it's pretty rude to just run off without putting out? You expect a return on your investment, is that it?

That's a very crude way of putting it, he says.

Am I wrong? I go.

I don't really mind that he's not the guy I thought he was or that he has more hair on the back of his hands than on his head or even that he's wearing this big tacky Rolex President, but there isn't a bed in the world that's big enough for me and his ego both.

You liked me in L.A., he says.

But I'm sober now, I go.

He pins me back against the door. I know you want me, he says.

I'm like, I don't believe this shit.

You want me, I can tell.

This is great, it's like, so typical, girls always think they're less attractive than they actually are and guys always think they're more attractive. I didn't want to say anything before, but really, this Bradley is a toad. He'd have to be really rich or really powerful or really famous to look even halfway decent. And even then . . .

Come on, I know you want to, he's going.

How can you tell? I go. I'm dying to know.

I know women, he says. I go, right, like I know Swahili. He's got me pinned against the door and then he latches on to me with his horrible bony little mouth, I mean you could get paper cuts from this guy's lips and I don't even want to mention his tongue, we're talking reptile, it reminds me of this diagram I saw once in a magazine about these lamprey eels that glom on to salmon and suck their insides out. Meanwhile he's trying to force my legs apart with his knee, I can't believe the nerve of this guy, it would almost be funny if it wasn't so disgusting, but luckily I've still got Jeannie's brooch in my hand. I open it up and sink the pin into Bradley's butt. He screams and jumps back like I'm on fire and while he's trying to figure out what happened I slip in the door and run upstairs.

I call Dean and get his machine.

I know how I'm going to get rich, I'm going to invent a device that will destroy answering machines over the phone—you just push a button and boom, the thing blows up.

I vaguely remember hearing Jeannie come and go early in the morning. A little after noon she calls me up from Hilton Head.

Sure enough, she walked in on Frank and some bimbo in bed. Everything that wasn't nailed down she threw at them. Then she went after them with a tennis racket. When Frank's new honey ran out into the hall naked Jeannie put her clothes in the trash compactor and compacted them into all the beer cans and watermelon rinds. This nice little Ralph Lauren ensemble, right? There was a champagne bottle next to the bed left over from Frank's big romantic evening and Jeannie clubbed him over the head with it. He was bleeding pretty nicely when she left and now she's at the airport coming back home. I get her flight information and tell her I'll meet her at the airport.

Before I leave I call up Dean and he answers. I explain about Jeannie and tell him I'll have to cancel. She's going to need me tonight, I go.

Hey, I understand, he says.

She's really hurt, I go, she's been screwed over. I know it's not rational but it's like I'm blaming Dean, maybe because he's a man, maybe because he was out when I called last night.

Give her a hug for me, he says.

And I'm like, what's that supposed to mean, honey pie?

And he goes, just a friendly sympathetic kind of hug. On second thought, he says, why don't you make that a nasty, frigid kind of hug.

So how was your night last night? I go.

Group sex and intravenous drugs, he says. Nothing special.

Special enough to keep you out past two-thirty, I think, because that was the last time I called before I finally fell asleep, but for a change I decide to keep my mouth shut. Right now my main concern is Jeannie. I want to be there for her because she'll be there for me when Dean and his replacement and the guy after that are all history. Ancient history.

# TWO LIES

I'm supposed to be on a beach again, imagining intense heat and sunlight. St. Bart's or maybe Southampton. The smell of salt and cocoa butter, the gritty feeling of a sandy towel. A really great method actress, I suppose, could get a tan this way, projecting herself into a memory of a beach. Then you'd know you were pretty good, I guess. But I can't even work up a sweat right now, at this particular moment. It's a Friday afternoon and I'm in class, trying to do sense-memory. My concentration's shot. I'm thinking about Dean. I'm heavy in lust.

Last night we finally got to do it. We went to a movie, then dinner. Couldn't keep my hands off him.

For some reason I was afraid it wouldn't be very good. I mean, I hate these big dramatic buildups, they usually let you down. Patience has never been my middle name, I mean I got my first credit card when I was about twelve, and if I can't have something right away I generally forget about it. But this, I don't know . . .

I wanted to crawl inside of him and stay there. I wanted to disappear down his throat. I wanted to take all of him all the way up inside me.

Trouble is, this isn't doing my acting any good. My instrument is all out of tune here. I keep thinking about Dean running his tongue up and down me, vibrations going right off the Richter scale, instead of about the hot sun on this stupid imaginary beach. If only the assignment called for a sense-memory of outrageously good all-night sex I'd be made in the shade.

I'm not sure why it was so good—we didn't do anything really special. No video cameras, costumes, equipment or special effects. Just good old-fashioned sex, like the kind Mom used to make.

Rob walks by my chair and says, you're not giving me anything, Alison. He gave me this assignment because last time I flipped out before I could get into it.

How about if I do something with sex? I say.

He lets out this big sigh and goes, you're going to make a great porn star someday.

What do mean, someday? I say.

Alex and I used to make videos of ourselves. It was pretty outrageous, but definitely a turn-on. I don't know, I suppose some people would think that's weird. I guess it is. With my luck the tapes will turn up just when I'm about to win the Academy Award or something.

The teacher goes, get back to the beach, Alison. See if you can keep your mind out of the bedroom for just a few hours.

So I make like Annette Funicello. I start with the memory of the smell of Bain de Soleil Number 4, remember the feel of the hot sun, skin getting really hot, hands rubbing Bain de Soleil all over my body. . . .

After class I call Dean.

Hey, big boy, I say.

Hello, beautiful, he goes. I made a terrific trade today.

It must be all that good loving, I say.

I guess you inspired me, he goes. I made two hundred thousand before lunch.

I'm like, do I get half?

Actually I made it for a client, he says.

I go, tell him I deserve a commission at least.

I'll give you a big commission, he goes.

I'm like, how big?

We're both driveling idiots. We sort of drool and baby-talk for a while, then I tell him I'm going to tan, then shower and dress and he says he'll pick me up around nine.

When I get home Jeannie says, Alison, I've got to tell you something.

I'm like, if it's bad news I don't want to hear it. I'm too happy.

You want a line? she says. She's definitely wired.

No thanks, I say.

Poor Jeannie, she's really wiped out over this Frank

thing. He's tried to call but she won't pick up the phone and she won't let me tell him when she's here.

So what's up? I go.

We got an eviction notice, she goes.

I'm like, I thought you said you'd cover me this month.

Yeah, she goes, but we owe three months.

Are you crazy? I go. I gave you my half for the other months.

What are we going to do? Jeannie says.

What do you mean, what are we going to do? What happened to the money?

Jeannie starts to sob. Oh, Alison, she goes. I'm sorry. Please don't hate me.

Get this, it turns out that Jeannie's been taking the money I've been giving her and her father's been giving her and spending it before she manages to pass it on to the landlord. There was this Chanel skirt she had to have, it's only like eighteen hundred bucks, and she's been flying first class down to South Carolina, and then she reminds me I participated in consuming that quarter ounce she bought a few weeks ago and there have been some eighths here and some grams there since then, just to keep her going. A new set of golf clubs for Frank's birthday—that was a real good investment. One thing and another.

So get the money from your father, I say.

I can't, she goes. He'll kill me. What about Dean? she says.

Right, I say. I'm going to hit up this guy I just met two weeks ago for five thousand dollars? Think again, babe.

What are we going to do? Jeannie says as she bends over the mirror and snorts a big line.

I'm going out to do the town with Dean, I say. Then Dean's going to do me. The question is, what are *you* going to do?

That sounds harsh, but I mean, *really.*

Dean has tickets for this hot play but first he takes me to Petaluma for a drink. The waiter's Mike from my acting class, he tells me that Didi showed up at closing time last night, really fucked up.

She was probably just waking up, I say. She's not really good till after midnight.

Girl has a problem, Dean says.

The play is *Fences,* I've been wanting to see it all spring and I'm definitely not disappointed. It's basically about how a father can screw up the life of his kid and I'm like, absolutely.

There's this one incredible scene where James Earl Jones's son spits in his face. My acting teacher told us that at rehearsals for the play the guy who was playing the son couldn't bring himself to spit in James Earl Jones's face so the director started to insult him and spit in *his* face and tell him that James Earl Jones was nothing special. Right. That guy's so powerful he's like the ultimate father where you can't tell if he's God or Satan or what, and when the boy spits in his face you think lightning's going to come down and zap the kid into ashes. Afterwards Dean keeps talking about the structure and character development and I wish he'd shut up, I'm just thinking about that moment.

* * *

After the play we go to Nell's. I'm looking forward to showing up with Dean, making it sort of official, you know, like—here we are, everybody. Okay, so I'm an exhibitionist. Of course, it could be dangerous. On any given night there could be eight or ten of my old flames slipping around in there.

My friend Whitney is working the door. Whitney was like Phi Beta Kappa at some Ivy League school, she was really straight, studied all the time and then she went to Columbia Law School but one night Francesca introduced her to this guy in Elvis Costello's band and she disappeared for about two weeks and now she works the door and does some modeling on the side. She has two big guys with her. She points to people and the boys pull back the rope to let them pass. There are about fifty people waiting. I feel bad walking right in, but what can you do? Okay, that's not true, I feel good. It's a mean old world, right?

Whitney checks Dean out, winks at me and goes, not bad.

It's pretty crowded inside, considering it's only midnight, but we get a table. A guy comes over and gives Dean a big hug and Dean goes, Alison, this is Phil, Didi's cousin. Phil's a big, athletic-looking guy. He's wearing a black T-shirt so you can see he's got this great young body but his face looks ten years older than the rest of him, like forty or something. He's got crow's-feet, wrinkles, skin that looks like it's seen a lot of wind from high-speed living.

And Phil goes, so you're a friend of Didi's. How is she? I haven't seen her in ages.

I look at Dean and he looks at me and we're both like, what do you want, the truth?

So I go, to tell you the truth I'm kind of worried about her.

What's the matter, Phil says, she looking for AIDS in all the right places?

You know how you don't like some people right away? Well, I don't know why but immediately I can't stand this Phillip.

She's been doing huge amounts of blow, I say. Every night, all night. She's got a real problem, I tell him.

Didi? he says, as if he doesn't believe me. Little Didi? I've seen her do a few lines but I can't imagine she'd really go crazy with it. What exactly are we talking about here? Because you're talking to somebody who ended up in detox for three months.

I'm like, good for you. I'm really impressed that you were such a major-league fuck-up.

Dean jumps in, he's such a diplomat, can't seem to stand unpleasantness between people, that's one of his big problems, he'd rather be pleasant than honest, I guess he didn't grow up like me where people were screaming and throwing cutlery at each other. Anyway, he goes, I've got to say I agree with Alison. Didi is pretty strung out.

Well, he goes, I'll check into it.

Hey, don't do us any favors. I'm really mad at myself for saying anything to this guy, and if he hadn't really pissed me off I would've made a joke out of it, but now I feel like I've betrayed Didi or something.

Phil makes like a tree, which is good because I could feel a major battle coming on. What an asshole, I say. What does he do besides aggravate people?

He's a stockbroker, Dean says. Relax, he says, and orders a bottle of champagne from the waitress with the soup-bowl haircut. I don't know, these downtown artsy coifs may get attention, but not necessarily the right kind. I don't think most guys are too keen on running their fingers through a fashion statement.

Anyway, suddenly I get a little tingle of tornado warning, like the air pressure drops radically around our table and sure enough a familiar voice screams *Alison* from a few yards away, then Francesca drops into the seat next to me, a natural freaking phenomenon—is that the word?—in green sequins and red beads. She's wearing this button over her tit that says THE DESSERT CART STOPS HERE.

I love Francesca, she's about the only person I know who has a sense of humor about herself.

My God, I'm so glad to see you guys, she goes, there's absolutely no one important or interesting here tonight, I was just getting ready to leave. Somebody told me Bono was here but I didn't see him. Hello, Dean darling, you're looking completely edible tonight. I'm absolutely starved. We went to some horrible Thai restaurant that just got a great review in the *Times,* me and Trey Burton and a bunch of other people and the restaurant had no bread. I told the waiter it's the fucking staff of life for Christ's sake. Can you believe it?

Rather ethnocentric of you, Dean goes.

You filthy boy, Francesca says, wash your mouth out with soap. She pauses to take a breath and do a quick surveillance of the room. Francesca is like one of those cartoon characters, I swear she can swivel her head three hundred and sixty degrees when she wants to see who's around.

Dean goes, so what are Mick and Jerry doing tonight, Francesca? I heard they were having a big party.

I take back all the nice things I said about you earlier tonight, she tells him. You're a jerk. When I have a party I'm leaving your name off the list.

Then just for good measure she turns on me and says, Alison, you're actually wearing a skirt and heels for a change. Did someone steal all your sneakers and sweatshirts?

It's true, I've got a little black leather skirt on, black silk top and decent heels.

And Cesca's like, you almost look like a grown woman. The way you usually dress, I mean, Dean may be a jerk, but unless he's really rotten in bed he deserves better than that.

He's fanfuckingtastic in bed, I say.

Go ahead, Cesca goes, depress me.

Have some champagne, says Dean.

And Francesca says, I don't drink, alcohol's got zillions of calories. Literally zillions. Later for you guys. I'm going home to try and scrape my makeup off. That's one way to lose five pounds quick and if I'm lucky it'll only take a couple of hours.

She kisses Dean, then me, then like a big green cruise ship she casts off her lines and steams away, blowing a kiss.

Speaking of weight, Dean says, there's no way you're a 34-B. He's wearing his extraspecial shit-eating grin, the one that he gets after a blow job.

What? I say.

And he goes, bra size.

How do you know what size I wear? I go.

He goes, I looked this morning before you woke up. You've got to be about three sizes bigger than that, he says.

I tell him, you don't know what it's like walking down the streets of New York alone with your tits. So I wear really small bras. It hides 'em. I can't believe you looked at my bra while I was asleep. You're weird, I say.

Dean and I are just getting kissy when suddenly out of the corner of my eye I see somebody ooze up out of the crowd and this familiar oily voice goes, Dean, how the hell are you?

Dean looks a little queasy, but I love it. I'm really glad to see Skip at this particular moment. I'm like, Skip, what a wonderful surprise. What an honor. I mean, gee, the great Skip Pendleton. Would you care to join our humble table?

Skip isn't exactly thrilled to see me, I don't think he realized who it was with her tongue down Dean's throat. But Mr. Polite takes a seat and tries to make the best of it. Dean's squirmy, but he offers Skip a glass of champagne and Skip says great! with this big fake heartiness. Men are so stuck inside these codes of behavior, they're like musicians who only know three chords. Emotionally they're punks. Dean and Skip are both playing at being good sports right now while mentally they're circling around each other like attack dogs. Skip's mind is going, I pissed here, this is my territory, how dare you piss here? And Dean's really upset because Skip got here first. So what does that make me, guys, the fire hydrant?

How are you, Alison? Skip says.

Never better, I say, looking at Dean.

Will you guys excuse me for a minute? Dean says. He heads downstairs. I don't know, maybe he's being nice and giving us a chance to make our separate peace or something, or else he's uncomfortable with the situation and can't deal with it. Or maybe he just has to take a leak.

You going out with Dean? Skip asks.

Yeah, I am, I say. He's great.

That's good, Skip says. I'm glad.

I'm thinking, sure you are, Skip, and then he waves to somebody on the other end of the room. He's always got his eye on the next thing, always checking to see if something better isn't just around the corner. He's ten times worse than Cesca. The only way to keep Skip's attention is to talk about him.

So Dean must've told you about the great time we had the other night, he says.

And like an idiot I go, when was this? I could've kicked myself as soon as I said it. Now Skip's got me. Whatever he tells me, he's going to know I didn't know it before. I hate to have him get the satisfaction of telling me anything about Dean.

It was wild, Skip goes. I think it was Thursday. I ran into Dean here about one. Neither of us was feeling any pain by that time, but we had a couple of bottles of champagne and then we went with our dates down to Automatic Slims. Had a great time.

I hear *our dates* and I know that was the whole point of the story but I'm not going to bite, I won't give Skip the satisfaction. He's going to tell me anyway. Thursday was the night I kept calling Dean and getting his machine. I woke up at ten and called and the machine was still on. He told me he'd been at a business dinner.

Skip's going, you know Cassie Hane, don't you? Nice

girl. Model. Not exactly a rocket scientist, but she's a lot of fun. I know Dean isn't really serious about her, though. Obviously he's a lot more interested in you.

I'm thinking, excuse me, Skip, but would you mind, like, stepping into an open elevator shaft on a high floor for just a second? I'm wondering if he suspects he got burned on the abortion deal. Or does he just think like three-quarters of the men in the world that any girl who sleeps with him should go to a nunnery afterwards and cherish the memory, or throw herself on a fire, or declare her vagina a national historic landmark and seal up the secret passageway forever after.

Anyway, he's out for revenge and he scored. He knows it, too. I'm so pissed at Dean I could cut his dick off. Not because he went out with this bimbo and probably screwed her. I'm mad because he lied and put me in a position where Skip could humiliate me.

My party's over at the front booth, Skip says. I really should rejoin them. Great to see you, Alison. Give a call sometime.

He winks in a way that makes me think he's serious. Probably he sees me as desirable again, now that Dean wants me.

This was definitely Thursday night? I ask.

I've already lost this round so I might as well get the information I need.

Let me think, Skip goes. Yeah, definitely Thursday, I had my tennis game the next day and I remember being hung over.

As soon as Skip clears out this guy Chuck Harnist sits

down and starts hitting on me. Like an idiot I slept with him one night so now he thinks I can stand the sight of him. Not that he's bad-looking, he could practically stand in for Tom Cruise, but when he opens his mouth he makes you wish you carried a roll of electrical tape in your purse. He's telling me about some stupid project supposedly in development with Paramount, like I could care less. Chuck's supposedly a screenwriter. He's one of these people who's always talking about deals, he's made a deal here and he's negotiating a deal there, but after you've known him a while you realize these deals are like a daisy chain where nobody ever actually has an orgasm, it's just a lot of lubricated friction. You sell an idea to a producer and he sells it to a studio and then the idea changes and then the studio changes and nothing ever happens except a lot of checks get written. Yada yada yada. Chuck has bored me to tears with this stuff a bunch of nights. Unfortunately, the last time it happened I was at his apartment when the drugs ran out and I was too lazy to go home, but if Chuck thinks I want to repeat the mistake he's out of his mind. I mean, it wasn't that good, honey. Frankly, I've seen bigger matchsticks.

So Chuck's yammering away and I'm thinking about how pissed off I am at Dean when suddenly I think, shit, where is he? Maybe he got really pissed off when Skip came over and actually left the premises. Or else he saw me talking with Chuck. He's kind of the jealous type, which is something I don't have much time for. I mean, what's the point? It's a lot of wasted energy, and my feeling when I'm out with a guy and I see some other girl hitting on him is like, great, if you can get him out the door, you can have him, I don't care. But first you've got to get him out the door, honey.

So I'm like looking around and thinking I better get rid of Chuck so Dean won't get all jealous on me and then I'm like, what's wrong with you, Alison? What do you care what that liar thinks? Dean's an asshole. Let him slink away on his belly like a snake. Good riddance.

Basically it's just that I don't want to be robbed of seeing the look on his face when I catch him up with his own lies. He can take a cab straight to hell as far as I'm concerned—I don't have to be lonely tonight, there's about eighteen guys here who would take me home in a minute. But I do want him to know that I know what a shithead he is.

Fucking Cassie Hane! That bimbo. That really pisses me off, I consider it a personal insult that I'd be placed in the same category as Cassie. A real smart girl, she's only a little less articulate than Sylvester Stallone. I mean, if he's going to fuck other women, fine, I don't mind, really I don't, but they better be at least in the as-wonderful-as-I-am category or how could he even consider it? Obviously the guy has no taste. That's what really gets me. If he thinks she's worth the price of dinner, how can he truly appreciate me?

Then I see him coming back across the room. I introduce him to Chuck and ask if he's ready to go and he says, sure, if you are. So I give Chuck this huge kiss for Dean's benefit, I can see him wince a little, he doesn't like that at all. You just wait, honey. Dean doesn't mind leaving early, though, because he thinks he's getting nooky. Dream on, babe. You wish. In the cab he kisses me and I let him. He tells me about some people he ran into on his way to the bathroom.

Back at his place he asks if I want a drink and I say no and he winks and goes, bed? and I'm like, sure, that sounds cool. Of course, there's bed and then there's bed, right? Like—you've made your bed, now lie in it.

When I come out of the bathroom he's lying between the sheets with his clothes piled on the floor. I turn on the TV and climb in with all my clothes on. He watches the last few minutes of Letterman with me but I can feel him getting restless over on his side. He clamps a hand on my thigh. Very subtle. When I start switching the channels he rolls toward me and starts kissing my neck and chewing on my earlobe, rubbing his crotch up against my hip. There's nothing sillier than a hard-on with no place to go.

I find an evangelical show. Brothers and sisters, Jesus loves you, blah blah blah. One of my mom's redneck boyfriends took us to one these things when I was eleven. He was a landscaper during the day and a stud at night and on Sundays he went to these religious revival meetings and blubbered about Jesus while this geek preacher healed everybody, casting out devils and throwing away crutches, shit flying all over the place. Eleven years old and even then I knew it was all a crock. This preacher was an amateur, I mean, give me a break, starting with my father I'd grown up around a better class of liar and cheater and con artist than this cracker. I've been lied to by the best.

Which reminds me. I suddenly go to Dean, he's kind of whimpering on his side of the bed, hey, I go, what are the three greatest lies in the world?

Is this a joke? he goes. He's definitely not into it. He's into getting into me.

But I'm like, no, not really. It's just kind of an old

proverb or something. You know. You're an expert on this subject. (This goes right past him.) One, the check's in the mail. Two, I promise I won't come in your mouth, and what's the third?

I forget, Dean says. I don't think he's trying very hard to remember. His eyes are glazing over. If you look closely you can see his IQ falling by the second. All the blood's draining out of his brain, headed south. Pretty soon he won't remember his own name. He's working his hand up the inside of my sweatshirt.

It's really bugging me what the third greatest lie is, but in the meantime I switch the channel to "Star Trek." Dean works his hand up under my bra strap and slides his hand in.

So tell me about Thursday night, I go.

The hand stops moving. Thursday night? he goes.

Thursday night, I say.

Was that the night I had a business dinner? he goes.

And I go, I don't know. Was it? You tell me.

I'm not sure, he goes.

And I'm like, maybe we should call Cassie Hane and ask her.

He lets out a big sigh.

Coming back to you now? I go.

He nods real slow and dramatic, as if he's a man who's been carrying this huge secret around with him for many long years through the rain and the snow and had bamboo shoots stuck up his fingernails by people trying to get this information from him but he didn't crack—and now that it's finally out there's nothing he can do about it so he's kind of glad to be relieved of the burden. I'm beginning to think it's Dean who should be the actor.

I say, why did you lie to me?

He's like, I don't know. I didn't want to hurt your feelings.

They're hurt now, I go.

I just . . . I made this date before I met you, he goes. I didn't want to blow her off.

You're a real sweet guy, I say, not wanting to hurt anybody's feelings. You're a real saint, aren't you?

I'm sorry, he goes. I guess I should've told you.

You shouldn't have lied about it, I go. I told you that's the one thing I can't stand. I'll be out the door so fast your head will spin. If you want to go out with other girls, fine. If you want to screw them, fine. But don't ever lie to me. Okay?

Okay, he says.

And wear a goddamn rubber, I say. I don't want to die from anything that comes via Cassie Hane.

We lie quietly on the bed, both on our backs looking up at the ceiling. It's the loneliest sight in the world.

Did you fuck her? I say. This time I turn and look into his eyes.

No, he says. He doesn't blink.

I don't believe you, I say.

It's true, he says.

I go, I'm not going to get mad at you. Believe me. I just want you to tell me the truth.

I just told you, he says.

You're lying again, I go.

No I'm not, he says.

Why didn't you fuck her? I say. Didn't she want to?

*I* didn't want to, he goes. I was thinking of you.

Well, you can forget about me for tonight, I say. Getting lied to turns me off.

I'm sorry, he mumbles.

I go, sorry for doing it or sorry for lying?

Both, he says.

So we do this manic depressive routine side by side in bed, both of us lying there like dummies for a while until we both start tossing and turning and yanking the sheets away from each other. Part of my problem is that I'm actually kind of horny. He got to my nipples before I let loose with the stuff about Cassie Hane. Finally I reach over and rub his hip, then feel for his cock, which gets hard in about three seconds, so I climb on top of him, slip it inside me. I hate to admit this but it feels good.

This isn't for you, I go, this is just for me. I'm still mad. I'm just horny.

He's not complaining. Dean may be a liar but he's not stupid.

# 7

# JUST CONTACT

Amazing, I wake up before Dean, drag ass into the kitchen and find some oranges in the fridge, an electric squeezer on the counter. Back in the bedroom I climb up and sit on Dean's chest. I take a big drink of OJ, then lean over and dribble a little on his face. His eyes flutter open. This boy looks scared. Guilty conscience, I'd say.

Did you fuck Cassie Hane? I go.

He's freaked. He turns his head both ways, then tries to sit up, but I've got him pinned.

I want the truth, I say. Did you fuck Cassie Hane?

Alison, he pleads. I guess he finally recognizes me. Was it the face or the tits, I wonder.

Did you? I go.

Yes, he says, I did. He looks away.

Thank you, I say, climbing down off him. Thank you for finally telling the truth.

I go in the bathroom and take a shower. The shithead has all the latest shampoos and conditioners, I'm beginning to think dickface is a little teensy bit vain. I went out with this male model once, the guy had more Chanel makeup than I do, that was creepy. Most guys' bathrooms *are* strange, though, even when they're disgusting they have a sort of impersonal, unlived-in feeling.

Some kind of weird black soap that stings my vagina, which is a little bit sore to begin with, granted. That will have to go. I'm an Ivory girl. If I ever decide to come back he better have my soap, plus a refrigerator stocked with my favorite beverages—Diet Coke, Amstel, Cristal. Flowers. I think Dean the liar is going to have to pay for this little adventure. Hey, don't ask me how I know, I just have this feeling.

When there's finally no hot water left I turn off the shower and use all the towels. Out in the kitchen, Dean's dressed and making coffee. He looks like the boy whose dad just got home from work to hand out the spankings.

He's got his table set with place mats and everything, a plate of bagels and Danish in the middle, little jars of English jam that he stole from some hotel, probably, the *Times* and the *Post.*

I went out while you were in the shower, he goes.

Well, isn't that special, I say, checking out Page Six real quick. I give it a lot of spin, a big shot of sarcasm.

But at least he knows who's on top around here.

I gotta go to class, I say. I'll see you around.

Will you call me? he goes.

I don't say anything, I just shrug like, if it occurs to me in the course of my incredibly busy social whirl and my active and fulfilling sex life, maybe, possibly, if I'm near a phone at the time and there's nothing good on TV.

The thing about acting is, if you're good you should be able to get all of that into a shrug. I think I did.

He's like, I'll call you.

If you want, I say.

So I go to class and knock everybody dead, I feel really great about my work, I do this scene from *Crimes of the Heart* with this girl in my class. I'm the Jessica Lange character, Meg. Rob tells me to work on my breathing and wants us to do it again next week, but he says it felt like I was inside the role. That's high praise from Rob. Then Carol—she's like a housewife from the suburbs or something—gets up and does a monologue from *Broadway Bound,* the one where the mom is talking about the history of her dining-room table. She's droning on and Rob's watching from the back of the room.

After a while Rob shouts, she's in the attic.

Carol stops midsentence, she looks like she's been slapped. She says, do you want me to go on?

Rob is like, you're not inhabiting your role.

So I'm not shy, I go, who's in the attic?

Haven't I told you that story? Rob says, even though he knows he's never told us, it's like this big mystery. So while Carol is standing up there in front of the class with tears forming in her eyes, Rob finally tells this story about how this actress—really talented, right?—married a rich guy who wanted to make her a big star so he was basically buying her the starring roles in these plays, like he would put up the money for the plays if the director would let her play the lead. So one of the roles he buys for her is Anne in *The Diary of Anne Frank.* Well, this bimbo was so bad that by the time the Gestapo came knocking on the door to take her away the one guy who was left in the theater shouts—she's in the attic!

After class I stop off to tan. Work on that golden brown look that makes the boys so hungry. Get home feeling great, pick up the mail, June *Vogue* plus postcard from an old flame who's in California now, wants me to move out there. "Remember that bench in Riverside Park? Love, Trip." Trip's all right. I don't know, some girls get love letters, me, I get lust postcards.

In the bedroom I flip on "Live at Five" to check out the news. There's an update on the garbage cruise story—this barge full of putrid gunk from Long Island that's been sailing all around the western hemisphere looking for a place to dump and big surprise, nobody wants the shit. Now it's just been turned away from New Orleans or something.

I check the messages—a worried one from Dean saying he's really sorry, he wants to see me tonight and he'll call later. I try dialing Francesca but I'm getting this weird signal, then a computer-girl voice comes on and says, we're sorry, your service has been temporarily interrupted for nonpayment and I'm like, shit, not this again, fucking Jeannie. I don't know, this happens every other month, just about, and suddenly I'm cut off from all my friends and delivery service from the deli. Trauma city. Last time it happened we moved into a room at the Plaza for a couple of days and charged it to Jeannie's dad while we waited for the check to clear, but after he got that bill he called the hotel and told them basically to shoot us on sight, or at least not let us charge to his corporate account. Between phone calls and room service I guess we did do some serious damage. Rebecca was in Paris for some reason, some guy, and we had the line open to France for most of the afternoon one time, taking turns with Becca while the other one went down to Trader Vic's for refills and all these fat out-of-town businessmen thinking we were hookers. . . .

That's part of the problem now since Jeannie's dad is really fed up and he's closed the vault. But it's like, these goddamned fathers, they give us everything for a while and then suddenly they change the rules. Like, we grow up thinking we're princesses and suddenly they're amazed that we aren't happy to live like peasants? With me it happened a while ago, Dad suddenly cut me off when I dropped out of college to come to New York, he'd been cutting down for a long time anyway, bouncing checks on me and shit like that, but Jeannie's dad just suddenly started cracking the whip a couple months ago and it's really cramping our style. Our first year in New York it was great, there were always guys around to pick up the tabs, and I'd just sold my Alfa for cash when I moved from Virginia, plus Jeannie had all the major credit cards. I admit we abused them a little. Jeannie's AmEx card was practically transparent it had been run through the little machine so many times. That was our idea of exercise, the gold-card press. Back and forth. So then her old man canceled all the plastic and cut her down to fifteen hundred a month, which is, like, what does he want her to do, start selling her body?

On top of everything else I've been thinking of tormenting Dean a little more, but suddenly the thought that I can't reach him makes me a little panicked. I mean, he can still get me, we're still getting incoming, right? But after fifteen minutes without a single call I'm thinking, shit, maybe they shut off all our service, the pricks. Dean might be trying to call now. What if it's an emergency? I could be dying of a heart attack up here or something with no way to get help.

The phone rings and I practically swallow it whole. It's Rebecca. She sounds halfway sane at the moment, she's over at the Stanhope with this guy Everett. And she's like, can you believe it, he's saying we've got to move to a cheaper hotel or something, turns out he's not so rich after all and he's spent his life's savings on me in the last three weeks. I guess it's sort of touching, but anyway, he's proposing marriage and he wants to have my children blah blah blah.

Story of Rebecca's life. What is it about men, you take a guy who's scared to death of commitment, who never makes a date more than two days in advance, you throw him in a room with Rebecca, who's probably the most unfit candidate for matrimony and motherhood on the whole eastern seaboard, I guarantee you in five minutes he'll be begging her to have his children. She's babbling on, saying, and then there's Manuel. . . .

I go, that little drug dealer that looks like Prince?

She goes, yeah, he's practically camped out in the lobby, it's really embarrassing, the doorman has to keep throwing him out and he waits for me on the sidewalk and begs me to marry him, he's quit drugs for me—can you imagine anybody quitting drugs for me, of all people? And he's quit dealing supposedly which was the only thing he had going for him in my book and now he's enrolled in some job-training program. All this so he can make a respectable woman out of me, buy a little house in Queens or something with a white picket fence. I mean, please. I told him that like ridding the planet of nuclear weapons would be a more realistic kind of goal, you know? Maybe start with that and work up. What is it with marriage this week, guys are proposing left and right, have you got the *Post* there, I should check my horoscope. Hold on, it's room service. . . .

When she finally comes back I go, Rebecca, what do you do to them?

Who? she says, her mouth full of something.

Men, I say.

Treat them like shit, she says. Everett's sitting here pouting at this very moment. . . .

Listen, I go, I really need money, have you got any?

Not really, she says, and she whistles when she hears how much.

I know she's lying, I went through her purse one night looking for cigarettes and came up with three Swiss bankbooks and two more from the Cayman Islands each with like five or six thousand in her name. I don't know where she gets it—guys, I guess—but she squirrels it all away in these banks all over the place and she's always crying poor.

What about Gran's pearls, she goes. You could sell them.

I don't want to do that, I go.

I'll buy them, she says.

I thought you were broke.

I mean I'll get somebody else to buy them, she goes. I have a friend who's in the jewelry business.

I go, which end of the business, stealing or stealing?

Gran's pearls are like this issue, I got them because I was her favorite and Becca has never forgiven me. She was furious. Since Gran died she's been sucking up to Pops so she can be in his will, but it's like she has this thing about the pearls, she wants them just because I've got them and Gran died before Rebecca could win her over.

Jeannie comes home and I tell Rebecca I gotta go and she tells me to think about the pearls, it's a triple strand of flawless twelve-millimeter pearls with a handworked platinum clasp. I'm like, yeah, I'll think about it. Thanks so much for the help.

When I hang up I tell Jeannie the phone's about to be cut off again and she goes, I know, we owe thirteen hundred bucks, and I'm like, shit, that's high even for us, were you and Frank having phone sex all month? and she's like, no, we were having phone fights all month. Then her eyes get all teary and I remember this is a touchy subject. I'm supposed to be sympathetic now that Jeannie's heart is broken.

Why me? that's what I want to know.

Alison, what are we going to do? Jeannie says.

You've got to call your father, I go.

What about your grandfather? Jeannie goes. He's loaded.

She already knows I'd never ask Pops for money. One of my principles is not to suck up to him, I don't know, he's like one of the few totally decent people in my life. The whole family is all screwed up but Pops has always been good to me and I feel like I'd spoil that if I started using him as a cash machine. Sometimes he sends me a check but I never ask and I probably don't write or visit as much as I should. Unlike Rebecca, who didn't have much time for Pops back when she was a kid, before she entered the economy in a big way as a major consumer. It's weird the way our childhood affected me and Rebecca—I find it really hard to tell a lie, it makes me nauseous, and she finds it almost impossible to tell the truth. Like everybody else in my family. But my baby sister Carol's practically normal, don't ask me how. So far. Sometimes I used to have this fantasy where I'd have Carol kidnapped by Australian bushmen or something and raised by them before she turned out like the rest of us.

Anyway, Jeannie knows I won't hit Pops up no matter what and I remind her.

You could always get another abortion, says Jeannie. Call Skip.

I don't know why, this really cracks us up, we both go into hysterics. I'm laughing so hard I'm practically crying.

Tell him the rates have gone up, Jeannie goes. Tell him it costs six thousand now.

We're like rolling on the floor.

I love Jeannie.

Why don't *you* get an abortion? I go.

But Jeannie says she hasn't slept with anybody but Frank and she never wants to speak to him again and anyway he wants to have kids, he'd just try again to convince her to marry him.

I'm like, Dean's feeling really guilty right now. He'd probably finance an abortion and throw in a free trip to Bermuda.

I fill Jeannie in on the whole Cassie Hane episode and she's like, fucking *men,* and I go, really. But after a minute I feel kind of guilty talking that way even though Dean's a liar and a wimp and a totally worthless shit, I really like him anyway. Jesus, I must be getting soppy in my old age or something. Next thing you know I'll be making goo-goo sounds and saying, *it's so precious* whenever a baby comes on TV. But don't hold your breath.

What are you doing tonight? Jeannie says.

And I'm like, I was thinking about letting Dean be my sex slave.

And she says, has he gone down on you yet?

And I go, that'll be my one of my first commands.

Let's make a list, Jeannie says.

And I'm like, whatever happened to my vibrator kit, anyway?

Suddenly the phone rings and we both dive for it and Jeannie gets it first but I pull it away from her and she's screaming in my ear.

So how's my little postmodern girl? Dean goes. That's what he calls me sometimes. I love it. Hearing his voice makes me real happy for about two seconds but then I feel a little pissed, right? because, you know, it's the same voice that lied to me. I'm being a little frosty during the chit-chat, so he gets down to important business, which is basically that Didi's cousin Phil has been looking into the whole Didi situation, I don't know how, and finally figured out that I wasn't bullshitting when I said she had a problem. Anyway, Phil already made an appointment for her with this specialist who's like the best in the world or something, but he needs our help. One thing he can't understand is where she's getting the money, he's talked to Didi's mother and father and they have no idea how she could be financing this big a habit—it's not like she has a job—and Phil wants to know if she's getting heavily in debt or fucking some dealer or what?

That's easy, I go. She was in that Pepsi ad about a year ago and she gets residuals. I've seen the checks in her purse, two hundred, four hundred, they come in a couple of times a week and she cashes them in about a nanosecond.

That's one mystery solved, Dean goes. The other thing Phil wants to know is who's dealing it to her. Does she have a lot of dealers or mainly one?

I can't tell him that, I go.

Dean goes, look, you want to help Didi, right? Phil isn't going to turn the guy in or anything. He just wants to call him and tell him not to sell to Didi anymore.

I go, Emile isn't like a social worker or something, you know. You expect him to just go, oh, dear, cocaine is bad for her, she's actually abusing it, well, that's very disturbing and I won't sell her any more?

Believe me, Dean says, Phil knows how to convince him.

I'm still a little dubious, I mean this seems to go against all the rules of friendship and drug abuse, but then I realize it doesn't really and if Didi winds up dead I'll be partly responsible, and Emile's a total creep and major reptile anyway. So yeah, okay, I tell Dean what he wants to know. But I also tell him that I don't see how in hell Phil's going to get her into rehab and I also say I'm really going to be furious if my name ever comes up. I know it's for Didi's own good, but I still feel kind of like I'm betraying her and I know that's how she'd feel if she ever found out.

So what are you doing tonight? Dean goes after we've taken care of the Didi problem.

And I explain to him that he's taking me out for an incredibly expensive meal and that he'll receive further instructions after he picks me up and brings me about two dozen long-stemmed red roses from my favorite florist.

We're still getting incoming calls a couple days later but I figure it's only a day or two before they cut us off completely. The landlord's lawyer has sent a letter telling us to be out by the end of the week. I'm like totally depressed. I don't even have subway fare. I'm so depressed I don't even go to class this morning—no way I'm walking sixty blocks, plus I just wouldn't be any good so I stay home and watch the soaps. When Jeannie gets in she's acting really weird, zipping around the apartment like a trapped bird or something, bouncing off the walls, tidying things, giving me shit for having my clothes thrown all over the place. Like, now what's her problem?

Finally she goes, Alison, I got my half of the money.

That's cool, I go. Did your father come through?

She nods.

Only half? I go.

My half, she goes.

Suddenly I don't like the way she's talking one little bit. Jeannie, I say, let me just point out for your benefit that I gave you the rent for March and April and you spent it. So let's not have any of this *my half* shit. If you're going to start using fractions on me then you better say my three-quarters or my seven-eighths.

Jeannie and the higher math. She never even heard of fractions until she started buying eighths and quarters from Emile.

Well, I could only get half out of my father, she goes. And that was on the condition that you pay the rest or else I have to find a new roommate. He thinks you're irresponsible.

I'm like, I must be dreaming. Has Jeannie lost her mind or is it me? I go, he thinks *I'm* irresponsible? Me? I didn't spend the goddamned rent money. Why does he think I'm irresponsible?

It was the only way I could get the money, she goes.

What was the only way? I go. Let me guess, you told him that I spent the rent money.

She doesn't say anything.

That's it, isn't it? You bitch, I go, I can't believe you'd do that to me. That's really the lowest.

It was the only way I could get any money out of him, she whines. He wouldn't have given me anything otherwise.

I'm like, you're such a liar, Jeannie. I'm completely surrounded by liars.

I mean, I know you can't trust men, and families are a lie from the start, based on the totally ridiculous notion that two people can be faithful to each other, but what else have you got in the world to count on besides friends? That's about it, in my book, and when your friends start lying and cheating on you, Jesus, it's hard not to be a total cynic.

It's like, you can't trust anybody, and if somebody you know doesn't fuck you over it's just because the price of selling you down the river was never high enough.

I'm sorry, Jeannie goes.

Just fuck off, okay? I go. I don't want to hear it.

Jeannie starts to cry. Oh, Alison, she blubbers.

She tries to take my hand but I push hers away.

I'll tell you something else, I go. If I ever fucked you over I wouldn't be a wimp about it and start bawling. If I ever decide to treat you like you treated me I'll know exactly why I'm doing it and I won't think twice and I'll laugh in your stupid face. That's the difference between you and me. You're a bitch but you're not even good at it. And you better be good if you fuck with me. Because when it comes to being bad, I go, I'm good.

Let her chew on that for a while. I'm out of here. I'm so mad I can't believe it.

I walk over to Dean's place which is like ten blocks but I don't have cabfare. I don't have shit. Thirty-five cents, four cigarettes and a barrette. Reminds me of that REM song, "It's the End of the World As We Know It."

I stop in front of a phone module, you could hardly call them booths, these weird little open-air units they have in New York now. Anyway, I call Francesca and get her machine—story of my life, talking to machines—which blows a quarter so now I've got like ten cents left. So I call Alex, my old squeeze, collect in Virginia. He answers and accepts charges and I'm like, I must be dreaming—something in my life today that didn't fuck up. Unbelievable.

Alex is like, Alison, what's happening?

And I go, what isn't happening? If it sucks, it's happened to me lately. I'm thinking of declaring myself a disaster area, you know, so I can get federal funds.

So I tell him about Dean and Jeannie and he's real sympathetic, I don't know, it's just nice to have someone on my side. We're best of friends now, I don't know what I'd do without Alex, jump out a window probably. When you've known somebody half your life and slept with them for a quarter, I mean—you get close. He knows me better than anybody. Same with him for me. He's family. Just ask Mom or Rebecca. They both were like, share and share alike. Popping up naked all over the place, like—oh dear, excuse me, I didn't know Alex was here, how very embarrassing, let me just very slowly cover myself with this teeny little towel after he's had a nice long look. I start thinking about this stuff while we're talking when he suddenly says, listen, Alison, would you be real upset if I came up to visit you guys?

And I'm like, that would be wonderful. And then suddenly I figure something out and I go, what do you mean, you guys?

And he says, you and Jeannie.

You don't even know Jeannie, I say. I mean, you've never met her.

I've talked to her on the phone, he goes.

You want to come up here and fuck Jeannie, I say. That's it, right? If that's the story, just say so.

I wouldn't even think of it if it wasn't cool with you, he says. Look, you sound upset, forget it, I'd never do anything to hurt you.

I don't know, at first it's like my stomach just drops out of my body and bounces on a little string just above the pavement. Alex was my first love. Hell, he was my only love and he helped me get over some things from my childhood, I mean when I met him my attitude about sex was what the early settlers must have thought about scalping—basically you'd rather be dead. Alex helped me over that, which is another reason this thing feels weird, him having the hots for Jeannie. If it were any other guy, no problem, hop right on. But then I think, well, why not, what do I care? If Alex wants to do it, he should, I don't believe in unrequited lust and it's not like we're going out anymore or like we have been for a long time. I can handle it, plus it would be good for Jeannie, even though I'm furious at her she's still my oldest friend on the planet and she hasn't been laid by anybody but Frank in years and just in case she's thinking of getting back together with him this should show her that a secure future with Frank is like two weeks in Philadelphia except longer.

Come on up, I say. It'll be good to see you.

I'll call my travel agent and talk to you guys tomorrow. Meantime, don't do anything I wouldn't do.

Which maybe rules out murder, obviously not much else.

I think Dean's doorman kind of likes me, he winks at me and lets me go right up. Guy's from one of those Communist countries that sounds like a disease, what's it called, where they used to have vampires and Dean's always loaning him money because he's completely in debt to these Korean gamblers who are going to kill him. Welcome to the free world, Igor.

Alison, Dean goes, when he opens the door. He's like, what a nice surprise. He looks a little worried, like he's got somebody in his bed already or something, but I guess maybe he's just nervous about where we stand or maybe it's my expression which probably looks like a psycho killer about now, anyway he lets me in, kisses me on the cheek.

What's the matter? I go.

I don't know, he goes. The bond market is really bad.

You losing money?

He nods. So here we are, two seriously depressed units.

The phone starts ringing.

How about you? he goes. Are you okay?

Oh, yeah, I'm just super, I go, really sarcastic.

What's the problem? he says.

What isn't a problem? I go. That bitch Jeannie . . .

The answering machine picks up and after the beep I'm treated to this silky lingerie voice going, Dean, it's Cassie, returning your call. I had the greatest dream about you, I can't wait to tell you. I'll be in tonight. Call me, angel. Don't leave a kinky message, though, cause Peter knows my access code.

Dean shrugs, looking helpless, like—can I help it if they throw themselves at me?

Can I get you something? he goes. He looks kind of scared.

I'm just standing there in the hallway trying to decide what to do, whether to just turn around and leave. And I'm remembering that Cassie Hane goes out with Peter Finnegan, which suddenly is giving me some big ideas.

Alison? he goes. Are you all right? What's the matter?

Fuck me, I go.

What? he says.

Let's fuck, I go. Let's just go into your bedroom and fuck, okay?

So we do. So I go in and lie down on the bed and he comes in and undresses me and plays with me. I don't play with him but he doesn't seem to mind—he better not—he gets inside me and I clench my teeth and grind against him and practically carve my initials in his back. I have my eyes closed, I don't even look at him, and when I come it's good but it's not enough, not nearly, he comes with a sort of a shout and rolls off. I give him about three minutes, then I grab his cock and start yanking—he better have eaten his eggs today, he's going to need them, I pull on his cock like it's attached to a busted cigarette machine and I'm having a nicotine fit, he winces and gasps through his teeth, then I climb on top of him and hump and ride, he doesn't know how lucky he is, the jerk, horsewomen have muscles he never dreamed of, doesn't deserve, and after about ten minutes I come but I keep my mouth shut about it, this isn't one of those beautiful sharing experiences, this is something else entirely.

Then he comes. Alison, he goes. Alison Alison Alison.

That's my name. My parents gave it to me, the creeps. Alison Poole. I'm going to make goddamn sure he never forgets it.

I try. I want this to be enough, just this. Just contact, just friction. But it's not. It doesn't fix me the way it used to, the way you always dream it will.

# 8 SCENES FOR ONE MAN AND TWO WOMEN

Get in touch with your child, Rob says at the beginning of class.

After our warm-up this guy does a scene from *Hamlet,* where Hamlet's trying to deal with the fact that his mother married this guy who killed his father. It sounds pretty good to me and the boy's really rolling, really emotional, and he has this great English accent, but Rob starts shouting at him about halfway through. He shouts, breathe! breathe! Your voice is up in your throat. Breathe evenly.

Finally Rob stops the guy, his name is Jim, and Jim's all sweaty and in tears and he starts wobbling around like he's going to faint and Rob says, what's with all the theatrics, all this huffing and puffing, squeaks and honks, it's all camouflage for something, what are you trying to hide?

So Jim looks real pained, he's trying to catch his breath and he says, I think I'm going to faint.

Rob says, you're not going to faint, that's more camouflage, stand up straight and breathe evenly. Okay, now, what's really going on here?

Jim shakes his head and shrugs and Rob goes, defense mechanisms.

Finally Jim gasps, defense against what?

You tell me, Rob goes.

Jim keeps saying he doesn't know and Rob keeps after him and finally he goes, this isn't about Hamlet and his father, this is about you and your father. It's all camouflage for feeling that your father wasn't strong enough, isn't it? Isn't that what's going on here?

Jim starts crying and finally he says maybe that has something to do with it. Rob thinks that the scenes we pick tell a lot about us. And I'm thinking maybe so, Jim seems to be really affected by this, or else maybe he's just playing along because it's a good scene, I don't know.

Acting's about honesty, Rob goes, after Jim has his cry. Don't be afraid of your feelings, he says.

So this girl who's new to the class raises her hand and she goes, I worry sometimes when I get into an emotion that I'll get totally carried away and I won't be able to stop.

Every natural emotion has a beginning and an end, Rob says. If we surrender to a predominant emotion in class it will run its course in a healthy way. Of course, he goes, if you're deeply troubled then you may not be able to stop and that *is* a problem.

Maybe it's my imagination, maybe I'm just paranoid, but it seems like he looks at me when he says this, I guess he's thinking about my little freak-out a few weeks ago, when I made like a spastic and had to go see the nurse. So okay, I never said I was normal.

Let me give you an example, Rob says, sitting up on his desk and folding his legs underneath each other—he used to study yoga in India before he decided to be an actor. Example, he goes, I sometimes have a fantasy of mowing down people on the street with a machete. I do. That doesn't mean I'm going to act on it. But it's something I occasionally feel. Not that I'm ever going to do it. A healthy adult can tell the difference between fantasy and reality. As a normal human being you recognize that you don't need to act on every impulse you feel. But as an actor you tap into the fantasy and use it. Of course, first you have to know the difference between fantasy and reality.

I raise my hand and I ask, how do you tell the difference?

He looks at me and says, Alison, have you ever considered therapy? I really think you should.

I'm serious, I go.

He goes, so am I.

So after this really wonderful day at acting class I get home to deal with the fact that my ex-boyfriend, the only love of my life, is arriving any minute to sleep with my roommate. This seems to me like a case where fantasy is leaking into reality in a serious way.

Jeannie comes home from work all flustered and excited

and I find out she's sent a car to meet Alex. I don't believe it, I don't mind her sleeping with my ex-boyfriend, really I don't, but we've got this incredibly serious deficit in this house, we're like Bangladesh or something, and she's ordering limos. I was down to my last dime until I made a little withdrawal from Dean's wallet. Foreign aid, right?

Jeannie spends the next two hours working on her eyes. Don't ask me why, but for some reason I think of this story I heard once about these two college roommates who hated each other—one of them was a friend of mine, actually—and one night she put some Nair hair remover in her roommate's mascara tube, you can imagine what fun that was.

Anyway, Jeannie's fixing her eyes, so I go down to the corner—my phone away from home. First I try Dean, no luck, then I try to track down my dad. I've got to get hold of some serious cash. I call his office in Washington and the secretary accepts the charges and tells me to try the farm in Virginia, he's down taking care of some horse business. Can I give him a message if he calls? she says.

Yeah, I say, tell him to get in touch with his child.

I'm kind of amazed that Dad's in Virginia because he hardly ever goes down there anymore, Mom lives there and they can hardly stand the sight of each other. You can't blame them, really, either of them.

Dad moved us out to the farm from Long Island after they separated, I was ten then. Before that it was a tax write-off. It's complicated, they're divorced and Mom still lives there but he owns part of it or something. It's a big white house with pillars, on a rise, seven or eight barns and stables spread out behind. It was a good place to be kids, all the land and horses. School was fifteen miles away and we'd always miss the bus and Mom could never get it together to drive us in, she was asleep most of the morning, totally zonked in her big pink canopy bed. When we were little we'd climb in and pretend it was a ship sailing off to England, where Gran was from, the chintz curtains were our sails.

I call the main house collect and Cliff answers. I ask if Dad's there and he says no. Cliff doesn't know where he is or when he'll be back. Mom and Carol are out shopping. I tell him to have my dad call me, then I hang up.

Cliff is probably my least favorite person in the whole world. He's Dad's right-hand man, he drives the car and beats people up or something. He tried to rape me when I was a kid. I was out in the stables and he cornered me, the only thing that saved me was I had the curry comb, I'd been brushing Eric the Red, and I finally whacked his face with it. I wish I'd hit him where it really hurt but I was so freaked out, his hands pinning me to the walls, and I ran like hell after I hit him. When I told Dad, he acted like he didn't believe me. And finally he said Cliff didn't mean any harm and told me to shut up about it. That's when I realized Cliff had something on him, that Dad couldn't afford to fire him. That's also when I realized that my father was a complete asshole.

I call Dean again and get his machine. Story of my life.

I don't want to be around to spoil the tender moment, Alex meeting Jeannie for the first time, so I fish out another quarter and call up Whitney to have a drink with her. Then I go back to the apartment and tell Jeannie I'll meet them later for dinner, but Whitney and I get really blasted and I keep trying Dean and getting his machine and so finally I go, okay, two can play that game.

* * *

The next morning I call up the apartment, I'm hung over as hell, and I check to make sure they're awake, I don't really feel like walking in on them when they're rolling around in bed, and Jeannie answers the phone all giggly like a newly minted ex-virgin or something and she says, Alison, come on up for breakfast, which is a zany idea, I don't think anybody's ever eaten breakfast in our apartment before. But then I remember, Alex loves the big breakfast production number, eggs and bacon and toast, the works, he'd cook up a storm most mornings, scramble five or six eggs just for himself, I'd be sitting there moaning over coffee and I'd say you're such a pig, Alex, and he'd say, I need my eggs if I'm gonna keep my baby satisfied.

I wonder if he said that to Jeannie.

I've got to say this is bugging me a little. Okay, I admit it. The funny thing is, I couldn't even stand the idea of sex, of having men touch me, until Alex.

He greets me at the door and gives me a big hug and even after everything it's good to feel his body and I know that I can forgive him, whatever happened it's no big deal, he's still there for me somehow, a way that Jeannie can't touch. He looks great, tan and dark and beefy. Jeannie kind of peeks out from the bedroom.

So, I go, when Alex finally lets go of me.

So what? says Alex.

You know, I say.

Jeannie says, I'm not the kind of girl who kisses and tells.

Right, I say, can I remind you who you're talking to here, I'm like your best friend and roommate, the one you always tell about your so-called kissing.

Let's eat breakfast, Jeannie says.

We decide to go out for a walk, Alex has never really seen New York, so we take him to Bergdorf's and make him buy us both some perfume. Then we go to Trader Vic's and have a couple of scorpions, we tell Alex about our wild weekend at the Plaza and then me and Alex tell Jeannie about the time we went to the Fontainebleau in Miami and flooded our room. Thinking about the weekend in Miami gives me a great idea, flooding the room wasn't half of what we did. Let's go to Forty-second Street, I say, and Alex is totally up for it, Jeannie's not so sure but she's really careful about showing it because she doesn't want it to suddenly become me and Alex again, she wants to stake her own claim.

So we walk down to Times Square. We're walking down Fifth and after a while Alex goes, what are all these people doing collapsed in heaps on the street? I guess we've been passing a lot of bag ladies and bums, and I'm like, I don't know, they're everywhere, and Jeannie goes, we've got a guy who sort of lives under the awning of our apartment building, which is true. When Alex sees the big black guy with the ski parka and the seeing-eye dog selling pencils out in front of Saks he stops and starts in on this big conversation, asking the guy where he's from and stuff. Jeannie's sort of embarrassed but I think it's cool, this is what I love about Alex, he's such a nut. Finally he buys a pencil and gives the man two bucks.

Alex is the total tourist, he sees the Empire State Building way down Fifth and he's like, wow, let's go up, and he's amazed when Jeannie and I say we've never been up it. So we promise we'll take him but first we go into this sex shop on Forty-second over by Port Authority after dodging all the drug dealers and pimps and Japanese tourists. There's five or six guys drooling over the magazine racks and they all sort of freak out when Jeannie and I walk in. Jeannie freaks out a little herself, she can't help looking like a nice girl from Princeton, New Jersey. Alex and I go over and start checking out the magazines, showing each other pictures and reading the titles. I pick up *Young Girls* and say, I'm going to buy this for my father.

And Alex says, yeah, really.

I can tell he's getting into being with me, we go back too far and too deep for Jeannie to understand and she's beginning to get a little upset about it.

I drag Alex over to the counter and make him check out the sex toys with me. The counterman is looking at us like he's afraid we're from Neptune or something. We start asking him to show us the stuff and how they work and what the features are. Meanwhile the perverts are slinking out of the store, they can't take it.

Finally we decide to get the four-pack vibrator sets, one for Jeannie and one for me, it comes with a battery pack and four attachments, the Super Stud, the French Tickler, the Rear-Ender and the Old Faithful. Alex pays. Anything to make my girls happy, he says.

We take Alex to Sardi's for a drink, we're trying to make sure we don't miss any of the touristy things to do. Alex wants to see some stars but the bartender tells us it's too early. The stars come out at night, he says and laughs like this is a great piece of wit. He's not bad-looking, though, maybe thirty, looks a little bit like Christopher Reeve. I don't even have to ask if he's an actor, you can tell from the way he talks he's been taking voice. He's overdoing the whole chest thing. We show the bartender our new toys and he gives us a free drink. When we're leaving he asks for my phone number, so I give him the Midnite Escort Service number, I memorized it for these kind of occasions.

Then we take a cab over to the Empire State Building and pay our two bucks and wait around in the lobby for the elevator with all these like families, moms and kids. Once we get on the elevator it smells like milk, I kid you not, and some little red-headed boy grabs my knee and gets gum all over my jeans. Freckle-faced, he looks like something out of a peanut butter ad. Another little kid starts bawling. I don't know, they talk about this maternal instinct, I can't say it's ever really hit me, but then I don't think it ever hit my mother either. I think she was just too lazy to put in her diaphragm some nights.

The ride up makes me really nauseous, my stomach gets left behind on the lower floors. We have to change elevators to get to the very top. Alex has his arm around Jeannie. She's telling him about her job and he's looking fascinated. It's really amazing the things we pretend to be interested in when we want to sleep with somebody. Sometimes I think conversation between girls and guys is all just foreplay.

To take my mind off how nauseous I'm feeling I say, hey Alex, what are the three great lies?

It's weird, he comes up with the same two I already know, except his second lie is a little different than my version, it goes, I promise I'll pull out before I come, you can bet the moms in the elevator are really freaked out by this conversation. But he can't think of the third one either.

Finally we get up to the observation deck and pile out of the kiddie capsule. I'm really dizzy. Jeannie and Alex rush over to the fence to look out, there's like this chicken wire all around the platform and blue sky beyond. The chicken wire's so nobody will jump, I guess, and it reminds me of this thing I saw in a book of photos from *Life* magazine, this picture of a car parked on the street, the roof of the car molded around the body of a girl who'd jumped from the Empire State Building. She was wearing a long billowing skirt that fanned out like a huge lily across the top of the car, the kind of dress you'd wear to a ball or a fancy dinner, she was lying face down so you didn't necessarily figure out what was wrong at first, it was as if she was resting or floating in a pool, a girl without a trouble in the world. . . .

I don't look, I stand right in the middle of the observation deck and throw up.

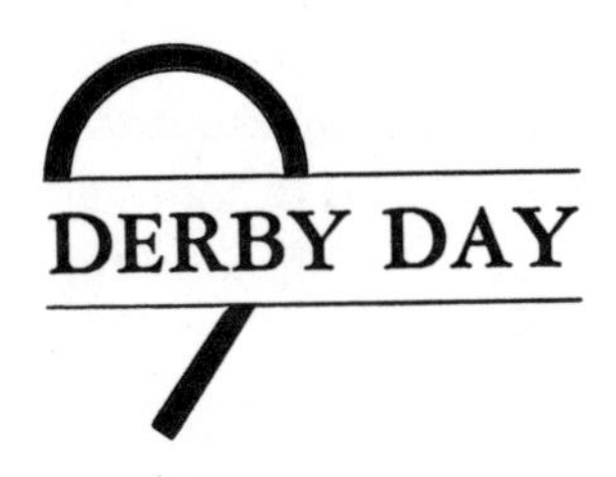

# 9 DERBY DAY

Thank God I never slept with Tom Walker. That makes at least one guy in the room.

We're over at Tom's place for his Kentucky Derby party and the past is coming back to haunt me. The gang's all here. I mean, I can handle it, no problem, but the guys are all acting weird. I never said I was a virgin, did I? Somebody tell me if I'm wrong.

I come with Dean and Chuck Harnist is here, and he's jealous of Dean anyway, Chuck starts making these cracks like saying he's redecorated his apartment and then going, Alison, you remember how ugly it used to be, don't you? The ceiling, for instance? And Dean says something about redecorating Chuck's face—for a smart guy Dean can act just like a dumb guy sometimes. But Dean's got troubles, the bond market's going to hell or something and he's really worried.

So Chucky's with some girl he must have met in Las Vegas, although actually she's from Texas, even her lips look like they've got silicone implants. Her name's Tina, but she tells me her friends call her Teeny, and she kind of looks at her chest when she says this and she laughs and jiggles her tits and that pretty much tells you more than you'd ever want to know about her.

And I go, yeah? Chuck's friends call him Teeny, too, but they're not kidding.

And she goes, wow, really? What a coincidence! And Chuck turns a nice salmon color and gives me this lethal look.

And then who shows up but Skip Pendleton, just the guy I wanted to see, and amazingly he's not with anybody. I mean, for Skip this is news, this is practically gossip, you know how some men wouldn't think of going out of the house without a tie, well Skip wouldn't think of showing up at a party without at least one vacuous bimbo on his arm. And he wears the girl for the same reason as the tie, for decoration. Maybe there's somebody here he wants to nail. I don't know, the only unattached women are Didi, Jeannie and Whitney and they're all my friends and wouldn't let him touch them with a ten-foot pole. Well, maybe with a *ten-foot* pole . . . I remember I read somewhere that outlaw guy John Dillinger had one that was about a foot and a half long and it's preserved in the Smithsonian or someplace. Now that's what I call the Washington Monument.

Skip is giving me these looks which I do not appreciate at all, these fuck-me eyes. And he's acting really strange with Dean, talking down to him like he's a kid or something, lecturing him about horses and race track society, which is really bugging me. Jesus. My old boyfriend, Alex, he told me this thing that guys say about girls—find 'em, fuck 'em, fight 'em, forget 'em. So if that's what guys say, how come these guys—these so-called men—can't fuck me and forget me? I mean why do they all have to act like crazy Latins afterwards, hot tempers and long memories.

Anyway, Jeannie and I are sort of friends again, but I'm still pissed off at her and unless I can come up with some money soon I'm screwed. The big news on Jeannie, though, is that she's madly in love with Alex. I knew this would happen. Apparently they screwed twenty ways till Sunday—Alex and Jeannie—and Jeannie figured out what she'd been missing. So now she's in lust with Alex, she thinks it's this great romance but I hate to tell her, Alex has this problem with his attention span and I don't think Jeannie's going to be able to keep him interested past yesterday. Meanwhile we've still got this money problem. Francesca's going to loan me a thousand, she's the best, but I still need at least a thousand more. She's at some celebrity derby party but she's supposed to meet up with us later.

Didi's boring the shit out of everybody talking about rehab. Cousin Phil actually managed to drag her in the other night. The way he did it was by keeping her up for two days, feeding her so much coke that she felt even worse than she normally does. Then he let her sleep for a few hours, then woke her up and wouldn't let her go back to sleep till she promised to go in the next day and talk to the shrink. Phil says the pre-op cost him about a thousand bucks in blow and three days' work, but Didi's parents are going to pay him back. So now she's seeing this shrink in the afternoon and going to group therapy at night. It's really great, I mean, here she is, more or less awake in the middle of the afternoon, and she's talking about her drug problem and how she's got to stop. She talks about it all night long, in between lines. It's a start, I guess.

From my point of view the only thing good that's come out of Didi's rehab is that she doesn't look quite so good as she used to, she doesn't necessarily look like a sex goddess the last few days, even though she's still doing drugs it's like something crazy has gone out of her eyes, the tension's gone from her body and it's sort of defused her looks or something. I don't know, maybe it's my imagination, but the guys aren't really flipping out over her today like they used to.

So Becca shows up at the last minute, right before post time. She's already called about eighteen times just to let us know that she's coming, finally she dances through the door in this micro lycra red dress—just a sheath really, perfect for that 3:00 A.M. nightclub appearance, but like even I wouldn't be caught dead walking around in this thing in the middle of the day. But the boys love it and it gets so quiet for a minute you can hear the sound of tongues dropping and saliva splashing on the floor.

Becca's dragging some preppy guy in her wake, all neat and tidy in his blue blazer and bright green pants, but he seems a little dazed. This must be Everett, pigeon of the month, the poor son of a bitch. He looks like a harmless version of Skip. I hope to God for his sake he's hanging on to his gold card for dear life, has his stock certificates locked in the safety deposit box.

Hey y'all, Becca goes, doing her southern girl thing for

the occasion. Who's winning? she says. What quarter is it? I just love these sporting events. They're so sweaty.

All the guys laugh. Am I like missing something, or is this funny?

The prep goes, hi, I'm Everett, but nobody gives a shit. Everybody's colliding and tripping, trying to give Rebecca a seat and get her a drink. Becca's obviously wired and it's only like three in the afternoon or something. Really sick. I wonder how much she's got.

We're all sitting around Tombo's loft drinking mint juleps in front of this big projection TV. Tom owns a gallery or something, I don't know, he's from Kentucky. Big ugly canvases on the wall, wacked-out Italian furniture, great bathrooms though, both with phones, I could easily live in the big one. Maybe he needs a roommate. Somebody young, blond and beautiful to answer his phone. Two out of three, anyway—I used to be pretty good-looking, way back in the olden days before Becca walked in the room.

I don't know, lately I've had this fantasy about moving in with Dean, you know, but I just couldn't see giving up my independence like that, it would practically be like marriage and anyway he's never asked.

Becca takes me aside and says, I can get you three thousand for the pearls.

And I'm like, not for sale.

Why not? she goes. You never wear them.

And I go, Gran was the only one in our whole family I ever liked. Gran and Pops.

Don't be a bitch, Alison, she goes, I'm trying to help you here.

Who's buying them? I say.

And she goes, just a friend.

I ask her if she has any blow and she says she just ran out but she'll try to get some more.

Right.

Becca's lie reminds me of this story I heard from a friend of mine who's a musician. He's working on an album with, let's just say this Famous Blind Musician, right? My friend's a session man, plays great guitar. So he's been up half the night laying down tracks with the FBM and meanwhile every half hour or so the FBM walks over into the corner and snorts from a vial—doesn't even bother to leave the room. Like, I don't know, because he can't see nobody else can? And after a couple times of this my friend goes up and says, hey man, can I have a blast? Because, you know, he's tired and all and they're working together all night. So the FBM says, blast of what? And my friend is like, a blast of that blow. And the FBM goes, I don't do drugs. Even though he's holding it right there in his hand. But I don't know, he's blind, so it's not like my friend can point to it and say, there! Well, this happens two or three more times, and the FBM keeps saying he doesn't have any. So the next time this happens, my friend finally goes up and taps the spoon as the FBM's putting it in his nose and says, if you don't have any drugs what's this? And the FBM goes—hey, you're right, what can I say? So he offers my friend some and eventually my friend says, why did you say you didn't have any? And the FBM goes, what can I say? This shit makes you lie.

Meanwhile, Skip's asking Tom if he has Trivial Pursuit and Tom says he doesn't and Skip goes, that's too bad, and then Whitney jumps in and says, yeah, I love that game, and just because I know that Skip takes like this great pride in his

Trivial Pursuit skills I go, Whitney is a really good player, and Skip says he's the best—the macho asshole—and Whitney, she went to Yale or someplace like that, she says, someday we'll see and Skip goes, I'd kill you. What a total jerk. I mean, as if we care, for one thing.

Shh, quiet everybody, Tom goes. We're coming up on post time. This old boy takes his derby seriously. Or at least he pretends to. I don't know, I think it's just a way of having a little bit of identity, you know? Like wearing suspenders all the time or collecting art or something. I mean, it seems like everybody's always doing something to impress everybody else. Anyway, he's got all these complicated bets going with the other guys and they're all acting very serious and involved, even Dean. The weird thing is, I don't think he even knew the Kentucky Derby was happening until yesterday when I invited him to this party.

I'm not betting, but I know the horse I want. I want Demons Begone to win.

So we've got these seventeen three-year-olds at Churchill Downs and there's some really good-looking horseflesh out there, all carrying a hundred and twenty-six pounds, I'd just barely make the weight myself now, but back in my riding days I was like, a hundred and two pounds, skinny as a whippet. And our horses were older and tougher, these three-year-olds have delicate legs, I hope to God they all make it okay, I can't stand to see a horse get hurt.

The other thing I hate is the drugs. Our horses were so pumped up and tranked down and wacked out they make me and my friends look straight. It was really depressing, but we were just kids, we didn't really understand. But we knew something was funny. We saw what they were doing and just learned to live with it. Drugs for pain and drugs for speed and drugs for when they'd passed their prime and they were heavily insured.

It's taking them forever to get this thing going, I mean the race only lasts about three minutes and they've got to wring all the advertising bucks they can out of this thing, plus give everybody time to get to the betting window.

Demons Begone looks ready, he's real feisty, dancing high on his feet. Skip's like insisting he knows for a fact that they've been holding back this horse Alysheba who's going to blow them all away. Trust Skip to have the inside dope. I hope his horse finishes last. Dean's so cute, he's picked this horse named Capote, just because it's named after a writer and he likes writers and wants to be one someday. What a dope. There's also a horse named Leo Castelli, but Tom the hotshot gallery owner isn't betting on him. Tom's going on statistics. Dean's a romantic, which is just another word for a flake, but I love it. I guess you could say we've made up, and then some. I just want to be with him all the time and I talk about him and think about him constantly.

I'm totally in lust again.

Finally they're off already after about nine hundred commercials. Demons Begone takes an early lead and I'm like, all right. Capote's on the inside and then Leo Castelli. Suddenly I've got to pee, must be all those beer commercials. I slide out of the huddle and Tom's like, Alison! as if it's sacrilege or something to go to the bathroom and I'm like, I'll be right back. I slip inside this big marble bathroom which is like the tomb of some ancient emperor or something and suddenly I feel real dizzy and nauseous, I put my head down on my bare knees and I listen to the shouting and talk from out there, it's strange how you can be involved in something and then just step back out of it and it seems really distant and silly. I suddenly wonder how long it would take them to notice I was gone if I went out the fire escape or something. What if I just kept going, left New York entirely? I'm getting this really weird feeling like, I'm so involved in all this hysterical noise which is supposedly my life but it doesn't add up to anything, if you step back far enough it's just a dumb buzz like a swarm of mosquitoes. But everybody's life is like that, right? It's like, down there in Lexington, Kentucky, the derby's the most important thing in the world to all these people, but what does it mean, really? It's just a stupid horse race, right? From the planet Jupiter, none of it counts for shit.

I don't know, I think I'm getting my period or something. Half the time I'm walking around feeling totally nauseous, and the other half I'm wasted, which probably has something to do with it.

When I go back everybody's jumping up and down and the horses are coming to the wire. What's with Demons Begone? I go to Dean and Dean goes, pulled from the race, talking like a telegram so he won't miss the finish.

Pulled from the race? I go.

So Alysheba wins, followed by Bet Twice. I don't know which bugs me more, the fact that my horse dropped out or the fact that Skip's horse won. It just figures. Skip always has the inside dope. I'm like majorly depressed. In between shots of the winner's circle they're showing Demons Begone being led to an ambulance trailer, hobbling, fucked-up, dead tired.

Bleeding from the nose, his trainer says. Sounds familiar, right? Jesus. Pour me another julep.

I told you, Skip goes, coming up and putting his arm around me in this creepy possessive way. You should stick with me.

I go, fuck off, Skip.

Hey, just trying to be helpful, he says.

I'm like, yeah, right. You could really help me a lot by diving out the fucking window head first.

Dean comes over and goes, I guess it was pretty stupid to think a horse named Capote could go the distance. He says, it's a case of sport imitating life—brilliant start, pathetic finish.

Skip goes, that *was* pretty stupid, Dean.

And I go, don't you call Dean stupid.

And Dean's like, whoa! Alison, cool out, it's called kidding. He puts his arm on my shoulder and says, a kind of verbal sparring characterized by irony and hyperbole that often passes between friends.

I'm thinking, friends! You don't know who your friends are, Dean. Sometimes I don't know what I see in him, really I don't.

Who else is holding drugs? Didi screams. Doesn't anybody but me buy drugs anymore? I know you all still do drugs, you cheap, sleazy bastards. I'm going to be so happy when I quit and you're all still addicted but you won't have me to supply you with free toot. The magazines say cocaine isn't fashionable but they really mean you fashionable fucks don't buy it anymore, you wait for me to come over . . . you invite me over to your house so you can do my drugs and look down my shirt.

I go, you're half right, anyway.

Dean says, hey Didi, honey.

And she goes, what do you want, Shakespeare?

And Dean says, I wonder if you could give me the name of your drug therapist. The man is clearly a miracle worker.

And she goes, Rome wasn't built in a day, asshole.

And Dean says to me, in this low voice so Didi can't hear, no, but it *was* sacked in a day.

I'm like, what's that supposed to mean?

He shrugs. I was just thinking about that basketball player, Len Bias, he goes.

I remember, a couple years ago maybe, that was the kid who ODed on coke and died. That was one of those times where everybody got all aroused for about five minutes and all these politicians shook their fat little fists and pretended they actually wanted to stop the drug trade and then Sylvester Stallone got a new girlfriend or Reagan got a malignant pimple on his nose or something so everybody could forget about the dead basketball player.

Didi says to Becca, are you holding? Becca shakes her head and Didi says, liar, I know you are. Fine, she says, don't give me any. I don't want any, I'm absolutely quitting tomorrow and then I'll be laughing at you when you're still a shivering wreck. Then she says, hey, I've got a present for you and she gives Becca the card I gave her a few weeks ago, the one with the cocaine help-line number.

This cracks everybody up. Except Becca.

Tom tells me there's a call for me so I go find the phone which is this weird piece of sculpture made out cement and plastic.

Alison, Francesca gasps, you won't believe it, guess who's here?

I go, Len Bias.

Who? she goes.

Okay, I say. Elvis Presley.

She's like, no, really. I'm dying.

All right, I go, who's there?

Jerry, she says.

Unbelievable, I go, but of course I'm thinking—big yawn. Score one for the bimbo patrol.

I've been talking to her, Francesca says.

Does she speak English? I go.

Francesca goes, she's in the bathroom now but I'm going to talk to her when she comes out.

I'm like, why didn't you follow her in there, see if she pees like the rest of us?

So Francesca gets mad and I tell her I'm sorry, it's just a really stressful scene here, my horse lost, Didi's nuts, Rebecca's a time bomb and I've fucked everybody in the room.

Jerry's back, she whispers. I'll call you later.

Meanwhile Rebecca's climbed up on the coffee table, she's holding this bottle of Jack Daniel's over her head and saying, let's party. She looks like some really kinky version of the Statue of Liberty and nobody's asking her to come down, all the guys are trying to look up her skirt . . . that's the way things are starting to go, and it's only about five in the afternoon. I have a feeling it's going to be a real long night.

# 10
# TRUTH OR DARE II

Reality is out the window by the time we end up back at Dean's place. It's like nothing can touch us as long as we stay high. Sitting down around the coffee table I'm having this déjà vu about a dream I had where Dean's living room is a stage and we're playing Truth or Dare for an audience.

Right after we walk in Rebecca's preppie asks what time it is—he's been holding on all night and he's probably wondering at this point if he's ever going to get laid tonight. Not that Rebecca hasn't already broken him in a little, I'm sure. Anyway, he asks the time and we all start booing and throwing pillows and cigarettes at him.

The usual suspects: Didi, Francesca, Rebecca, Skip, Ev the Prep and Dean. Jeannie crashed, I think Alex wore her out last weekend and I guess we lost Tom and Whitney at Nell's. Chuck and Teeny we ditched, said we'd meet them at some dumb restaurant where they were actually going to eat. Seems like days ago.

I'm like a shivering wreck. Totally nauseous.

The coffee table is full of beer and champagne bottles and there's three or four mirrors going around. And suddenly Didi goes Truth or Dare and that snaps me back into the real world in about a nanosecond. I'm like, uh-oh. Not a good idea.

Dean says, yeah, great idea, the horny bastard must want to see Didi's tits again. And Rebecca's all for it too, she's an exhibitionist from way back.

I take a quick look at Skip and he's looking back at me and I don't like his eyes one little bit. And I'm thinking, whatever those two things are you weren't supposed to ever mix together in chemistry class, they're about to get poured into the same beaker.

So the next thing I know we're in the middle of it and I am not a happy unit, I'm sweating bullets.

Of course Didi has to start, and of course she has to make trouble, so she picks Skip, who takes truth and Didi goes, two parts, how would you rate Alison in bed and, part two, did she go down on you?

Skip's loving this. But Dean isn't and neither am I. Finally Skip goes, I'd give her a nine.

What about part two? Didi goes, and I can see Skip isn't so keen all of a sudden because the fact is I didn't and if I weren't here the liar would go ahead and lie about it, but now he can't and he kind of shrugs his shoulders and says no.

Rebecca says, I can't believe Alison's a nine.

And Francesca goes, especially without going down on him.

Skip's turn, Didi shouts.

Me, me, Rebecca says. Pick me.

Okay, Skip goes, and of course Rebecca takes the dare and of course Skip goes, take off your clothes. So Rebecca jumps up and strips down, the guys are stunned and silent like they're in church or something while Becca shakes her booty, I've got to admit it's a nice package, you'd think she worked out about nine hours a day, if I were a guy I'd fuck her in a minute, it's a toss-up whether she or Didi has a better body, and finally the guys start giggling nervously and Becca puts her clothes back on real slow.

So then it's Becca's turn and when she goes Dean, he picks truth of course, the guys almost always pick truth. And Becca says, do you have a hard-on right now? and Dean says yes. Big surprise, with Dean all you have to do is like say the word nipple or something and he's ready to bust out the front of his chinos. Story of his life. Maybe he didn't get enough when he was younger. He told me he had a practically permanent hard-on from the age of thirteen to sixteen and how he used to get really nervous when class was ending because he wouldn't want to stand up and walk down the hall with an erection so he'd try to think about violence and garbage and stuff like that or else he'd sit in his chair like a moron and pretend he was rearranging his notebook or something.

So Dean picks Skip and I'm like, uh-oh. He says, do you still have the hots for Alison?

More specific, Didi says. Vague question.

Okay, Dean goes. Would you sleep with her again?

Skip goes, would I? Really smug, he smiles and finally says, you bet. And he and Dean lock eyes for a minute and I'm dying, I don't like what's happening here at all.

So Skip turns to me—I pick truth, I'm only a private exhibitionist—and goes, does Dean really satisfy you sexually?

And I go, yes, he does.

Skip leaves it at that, but he has this look like he just scored a point.

Boring, says Didi. She's vibrating at this really high frequency. Suddenly I notice this incredible thing—Dean has this weird expression, he's sitting on the floor with his legs under the coffee table and Rebecca is slumped in this really low chair right next to him and I see her reach down under the table and from Dean's expression it's like obvious that she's grabbed hold of his crotch. Dean has this slightly queasy expression when he looks up and sees me and I'm thinking, this can't be happening, but with Becca it definitely could be happening. She looks right at me, then lifts up her arm and sits back up in her chair with this ridiculous innocent look.

So I go to Rebecca, truth or dare, do you like the idea of seducing my boyfriends or is it just something that happens sometimes?

She goes, only if I find them attractive.

Good, says Didi. High reality quotient in that question and answer.

And I'm thinking about the time we were all sitting around in the hot tub in East Hampton, somebody's father's house, whatever poor bastard Rebecca was sleeping with that week, me and Alex, Rebecca and her squeeze, this was like two years ago when Alex and I were still going out, we were practically married for Christ's sake, it had been almost four years or something. Anyway, we're all in that condition where you can't tell where the water stops and you begin, it's all like the same warm ooze, the four of us in the hot tub drinking Cristal wrecked on Quaaludes and we're like joking around about having an orgy and the next thing I know I feel a hand fishing around between my legs, I mean it could be anybody but I figure out it's what's-his-name, Trent, that was his name, and suddenly Alex is grinning and squirming around and we were all doing this underwater foreplay and it was cool, we were all friends and that was the point, and Alex is touching me too but it's just sort of giggly and casual. So like a jerk I decide to get up and take a pee, don't ask me why I didn't just pee in the water, so we're out in this kind of cabana deal and I have to get out and go to the bathroom next door. And I guess it takes me a while to find it or maybe it takes me a while to get the door open—I don't know, we were pretty fucked up at this point. I was, anyway, my whole body felt like a waterbed, so finally I get in and I'm just like washing my hands or something when the door opens and it's Trent, who's got this monster hard-on sticking out in front of him, I remember it cracked me up, like how can you walk around with that and not feel totally ridiculous? I remember thinking some things are meant to stay underwater, you know, and then Trent grabs me and sticks his tongue down my throat and I'm like, hey, we're outside the theater now, this script doesn't apply out here in the lobby and meanwhile Trent's trying to get my legs apart with his knee, I'm standing backed up against the sink and I pulled my face away and spotted the light switch just at that minute, it was this naked man made out of plastic and like the up-and-down switch was his crotch, very tasteful, right?—and it just sort of fit in with everything else. I kneed Trent in the balls and said, fuck off, I'm going to tell Rebecca if you don't chill out and he goes—holding his nuts and moaning—she doesn't give a shit, what do you think she's doing right now? and suddenly I'm running out to the hot tub and it's empty, there's no one there and I run up to the house, I rush up the staircase following these wet footsteps that get fainter and fainter and then disappear, I'm out of my mind, I start ripping open the bedroom doors, of course there are about twenty bedrooms in this goddamn house. I find them in Rebecca's room, they haven't even pulled the sheets up over them, I see Rebecca's face underneath him looking out at me like she was expecting me, her mouth open and glistening like something horrible coming up from the bottom of the ocean. . . .

Some impulses you should stifle, right? I never used to think so, I've always done whatever I felt like, I figured anything else and you're a hypocrite like I told Dean, but I don't know, here in the middle of this really ugly Truth or Dare session watching my sister grab my boyfriend's dick, thinking about her and Alex back then, thinking about some of the shit I've done recently, I'm beginning to wonder if a little stifling is such a bad thing. Right now I'd give my grandmother's pearls for a little white lie. The way this game is going, I'd give all my possessions for a dose of amnesia.

So I get up and go to the bathroom while Truth or Dare is raging around me. This is even worse than the fucking derby.

After a minute Dean knocks on the door and asks me if I'm okay.

It's all right, I say.

But actually I'm feeling like shit. I'm a shivering wreck, drunk and high and totally nauseous. I sit on the toilet for about ten minutes with my head on my knees, then I go back out.

Alison's looking wasted, Becca says.

A shivering wreck, Didi says.

She needs help, Becca goes. She hands me this ratty little card, I have to look real hard to focus on it. Big letters, H-E-L-P. Becca starts singing a chorus of "Help me, Rhonda" and Didi joins in for a second, then says, Ev-er-ett, tell the truth . . . how many girls?

Approximately twenty, says the prep.

Exact figures, Didi says. No rounding off.

Maybe twenty-two, he goes. By now the prep is looking really miserable and who can blame him?

So then he asks Dean, truth or dare.

And Dean says, I think I'll keep my clothes on, thanks. He picks truth.

No fair, Becca says. We want full frontal male nudity.

Everett says to Dean, am I crazy or did I see Rebecca grab your, uh, you know?

You ain't crazy, Dean says. He has this stupid smile.

God, Francesca says, I missed that.

Rebecca turns and looks at me. I was just checking his answer when he said he had a hard-on, she explains.

Rebecca the fact chekka, says Francesca.

It's Dean's turn, Everett says.

And when Dean says my name, I don't like the tone of

voice. He gives me this really unpleasant look. Truth or dare? he goes.

Truth, I say. I should've taken the dare.

And he says, have you slept with Skip recently?

I go, recently?

In the past week, he says.

I don't think I've ever wanted to lie so much in my life. But Skip's right here and he's not going to let me get by with it.

Didi, smelling blood, starts going, truth, truth, truth!

Everybody else gets real quiet.

Yeah, I say.

I look up at Dean, his eyes are this beautiful soft blue that sometimes looks like a tropical ocean. But now they look so cold.

I want to explain. I'd really like to tell him about it, I think I could make him understand. Not that I'm proud of myself.

Well, well, well, says Rebecca.

There's a knock on the door, which is great, anything to break this mood, a mass murder would make a nice change in the atmosphere here and Dean says, shit, probably my neighbor bitching about the noise. His voice is a little shaky but he's probably really glad to have the distraction of something normal to deal with because I can tell he's really upset and it's like breaking my heart. I don't think he expected me to say yes, he was just suspicious.

So Dean gets up to go to the door and Francesca is shaking her head like she hates to see her friend fuck up so bad, then she suddenly looks over toward the door and lets out this shriek and Skip goes, what the fuck! and Rebecca is like, oh Jesus, give me a break, Mannie.

Sure enough, it's the guy we supposedly rescued Rebecca from up in Morningside Heights last month or whenever it was. Except I think it was the other way around. He's got his knife out again. I don't know, it seems kind of harmless at this point, like sort of a gimmick, you know, his schtick. Some guys wear suspenders, Mannie the drug dealer always carries a knife.

He looks all hopped up, except Rebecca said he'd quit doing drugs so he could get a job and make an honest woman out of her, fat chance of that. And he's wearing a suit and a tie which seems weird, he doesn't look like he's used to it, he basically looks like he dressed up to visit his grandmother's house or maybe to try and impress the folks down at the immigration office.

He sort of zigzags into the room, crouched down low with the knife out in front of him, the way cops move on TV when they're expecting gunfire any minute.

Cut the theatrics, Mannie, Becca says.

And Mannie goes, you loved me.

I fucked you, she says. There's a difference.

Hey, what's this all about? Everett goes.

I got a job, Mannie says. You were going to live with me.

That was your idea, she says, not mine.

Come back, he sobs. There are actual tears running down his cheeks. He lowers the knife, which he's been pointing at Didi, lets his arms fall to his side. Please come back, he goes. It's really pathetic.

It was only one night for Christ's sake, Becca says.

Two nights, says Mannie. I never will forget.

Rebecca's like, whatever.

Obviously it didn't make quite as unforgettable an impression on her.

I guess he rates you a ten, says Didi, who keeps chopping lines like she sees this sort of thing every night.

Wait a minute, I want to know what's this about, Everett goes. He stands up and says, whoever you are, I think you better leave. Now. He looks at Rebecca for support.

He can do whatever he wants for all I care, she says, watching Didi lay out the lines.

Look buddy, why don't you give me the knife? Everett says. He's a pretty big boy, six two or so and built, I mean he probably played lacrosse at Dartmouth and this guy Mannie's about a foot shorter.

I don't know what happens next—the prep makes a move and Mannie freaks, suddenly the prep is holding his arm and there's blood dripping out from between his fingers.

Oh God, Francesca says.

Dean's been watching this, he's seen Mannie in action once before so he wasn't too worried at first, I guess, but now he comes up toward Mannie and says, look, give me the knife, Mannie. You know me, he says, I'm not going to hurt you, and just then Everett goes, I'm going to hurt you, you motherfucking spic, you cut me. And Mannie's looking like a trapped animal, I really feel sorry for the little guy, he's just confused.

He backs himself up against the window, pointing the knife at Dean and the prep, his arm whipping back and forth like a dog's tail. He kind of climbs up onto the windowsill and Dean's going, Mannie, calm down, okay? Let's talk about this thing.

And Mannie, he's breathing like a horse after a race, gasping for air, and he goes, please, Rebecca, I love you. Please.

God, the sound of his voice, this despair, it's like the saddest thing I've ever heard in my entire life, practically.

Rebecca leans over the mirror and snorts a line.

I'll hurt myself, Mannie screams.

Be my guest, says Rebecca.

Come on, Mannie, Dean says, real soothing, there's this big drama going on but of course I'm thinking about myself, I'm thinking about Dean, what a sweet guy he is, basically. I'm really proud of the way he handles things, unlike Skip, and I'm thinking, shit, maybe I've blown it forever, and all this is going through my head in about three seconds.

Then Everett makes another try for the knife.

Mannie screams Rebecca's name and then I don't know, suddenly he disappears, he's just gone, and Dean rushes over to the window and looks out. Oh God, he says, oh Jesus.

Everett is just standing there in a daze, bleeding and saying, he cut me, then Skip looks out, he doesn't say anything, he runs from the window to the coffee table and grabs Didi's bag and says, quick, we've got to flush this stuff before the police get here and I'm still having trouble catching up with the situation, I'm like—the police?

It takes me a minute to realize we're on the sixth floor and Mannie's jumped out the window.

# 11 HUNTERS AND JUMPERS

So when Francesca calls I'm asleep as usual, I can't seem to wake up anymore. I could sleep forever. But I'm half dreaming and I hear Francesca's voice on the machine and she was already in the dream but the voice keeps saying pick up pick up and I'm thinking what did I drop, what did I lose, pick what up? Then I wake up enough to figure out it's the phone.

What? I go.

Alison, I don't believe it, I've been leaving messages on your machine for two days, where have you been? and I go, I've been sleeping.

With who? she says and I don't say anything.

Listen, she goes, you won't believe it, you will never in a billion years believe where I was Thursday night.

I'm like hanging on, holding my head and rubbing my eyes, and she goes *Alison,* really impatient, and I realize I'm supposed to act interested so I ask where.

Mick and Jerry's, she goes. Do you believe it?

I don't believe it, I say, like I could give a shit. I mean I'm glad she's happy but right now I have this headache and I'm feeling nauseous and I could give a shit about lifestyles of the rich and infamous. I'm a lot more worried about survival of the fittest, and like whether I'm going to make the cut or join the club for dinosaurs and dodo birds.

I feel like shit.

Francesca says, it was so great, guess who I sat next to?

I pretend to listen for a while and then I tell her I gotta pee and swallow some aspirin, I'll call her later and I can tell she's kind of ticked that I'm not having multiple orgasms about her social coup, but I just don't care right now, so shoot me.

Maybe because she's mad at me she says, I saw Dean at Elio's last night.

I know there's more coming. Yeah? I go.

She goes, he was with his old girlfriend, Patty.

For some reason this doesn't surprise me. In fact, as soon as I hear it I feel like I already knew it.

When I don't say anything, Francesca says, he was a jerk.

Dean's not a jerk, but I don't feel like arguing.

Then suddenly I go, Francesca, what's the third great lie?

She's like, huh?

What's the third great lie? I go. The first one is the check's in the mail. Then, I promise I won't come in your mouth. What's the third?

But she doesn't know either. I tell her I'll call her back later.

I almost fall back to sleep but instead I get up and lurch to the bathroom, using the walls for support. I suck down three Extra-Strength Tylenols and then I look at my face in the mirror, it's all puffed out and blotchy, my tan's shot, my eyes look Chinese. I stand there for a while holding onto the sink feeling like I could puke, but it doesn't quite come.

The phone's ringing again, I forgot to turn the machine back on. For some reason I answer and it's Whitney. Alison, she goes, you'll never believe it (I'm like, why is everybody so sure I won't believe them, at this point I'll believe fucking just about anything), I was working the door last night and who shows up but Skip Pendleton with some thirteen-year-old bimbette on his arm. Well, you remember how he said he was such an expert at Trivial Pursuit and he'd kill me if we ever played? So he's like standing outside the rope expecting me to sweep him right in and I go, Skip, what's the year the Beatles first played Hamburg and what's the name of the club they played? and he's like, what? And I say, Trivial Pursuit, Skipper, and he says, I don't know and I say, sorry, then, you can't come in. He almost died, he's just standing there and I wouldn't let him in . . . I didn't . . .

She goes on and on and I'm thinking she sounds like an idiot. Yada yada yada. God, she sounds just like me. A few weeks ago this story would've had me rolling on the floor and slapping my ribs but now I'm hardly listening.

Isn't that great? she finally says.

I go, just great.

I knew you'd love it, she says.

That story is going to change my fucking life, I say.

Hey, I just thought you'd be interested, Skip and all, she says. No need to be such a bitch.

I tell her I'm sorry, I'm just sitting here desperately waiting for my period, I'll call her later when I'm feeling human again, though frankly if I never saw Whitney again it wouldn't bother me for more than a nanosecond.

I don't know, I don't seem to want to have anything to do with anybody who was there that night. But then, I don't seem to want to have anything to do with anybody, period.

It's been almost two weeks. I've only talked to Dean twice since then, once the morning after when he was at the hospital. He called to tell me that Mannie was stable but critical, whatever that means. About a week later I called him back. It was really awkward. We tried to make small talk. He said he'd talked to Phil and that Didi had been clean since the accident and she's started going to some church group down in Soho and she never wanted to see another line of cocaine in her life. I knew that already, I've been hearing about it day and night whenever I'm not crashed out sleeping. She calls me and preaches, which is probably why I'm so sleepy. It's all she can talk about, how bad she was then and how glad she is now that she's stopped and how Jesus is the man with the plan. Amazing Grace, how obnoxious the sound. I think I liked her better as a junkie. But I said to Dean, oh yeah? like I didn't know all this, because I wanted to talk to him and I didn't want him to hang up and we needed something besides ourselves to talk about. That's good, I said. Everett got a few stitches in his hand, Dean said. And he told me the police had closed their investigation.

They questioned all of us, and our stories were pretty much the same. At first they were sort of nasty about it, when they clumped in, it was obvious we were all fucked up, but by that time the premises were drug-free. What clinched it was when Mannie regained consciousness, he said it was his own fault. He said he'd meant to scare his girlfriend and that he'd slipped on the windowsill. Could've happened to anybody, right? In the meantime there'd been a few million new crimes in the naked city so the cops were happy to drop it. The whole thing was only a paragraph in the *Post* and the *News,* about how some nobody fell out of a window on the Upper East Side and lived to tell the tale. Jesus. Skip got twice the column space the last time he threw a party.

Rebecca split town the day after. She tried to leave the apartment before the cops got there but Dean wouldn't let her. The next day she was gone, I know because Everett called here looking for her. He told me he got five stitches where Mannie had cut him. A couple nights ago there was a crackly message on my machine from Rebecca in Lugano, Switzerland, where she's staying in this incredible hotel overlooking the lake, drinking champagne and eating radioactive chocolate. She said she's totally in lust, she'd met a great new guy. Story of her life.

Jeannie's in South Carolina visiting Frank. They reconciled after Alex called up and said he couldn't make it for the weekend and that he didn't think he'd be up the next weekend either. Jeannie's been working late and checking out china and silver patterns during lunch and I've been sleeping most of the time so we haven't really talked much lately, I'm not sure what's going on in her mind. It looks like I'm going to have to find a new place soon since her old man thinks I'm irresponsible and that the two of us are a dangerous combination. It's not really Jeannie's fault, I guess. She says I can stay as long as I need to find a new place, but Francesca told me I could move in with her and I guess a change is as good as a rest.

A few days ago some friend of Rebecca's called up, he said he was a jewelry dealer and that he wanted to buy the pearls, so I'm going to take them over tomorrow, I don't know what else to do.

My father says he's broke. Which is total bullshit but what can I do? Can you sue your father for nonsupport? He sent me a check for five hundred dollars—like wow, thanks Dad—but that was gone before I'd even cashed it. I owe everybody. The last thing Dean said to me was, do you need money? and like an idiot I said no.

I know, I've got to get a job, I guess I'll have to waitress—God how depressing, but right now I'm having trouble getting out of bed, I haven't even been to class in a week. Tomorrow after I go meet this so-called jewelry dealer I'm going to the doctor. I'd probably feel better about myself if I could go and work on my instrument, but I feel too shitty to bother, it's a vicious circle. Or is it cycle? Dean used to tell me these things. A few more months with him and I might even have started to feel educated.

Dean said he was buckling down to his work, really getting organized, going to bed early and waking up early, keeping a journal and working on some ideas for plays. I could tell that was kind of directed at me—blaming me for his wildness. There was this big slide in the bond market a few weeks ago and it really freaked him out, he's like a reformed sinner or something. It suddenly occurred to him they might show him the door before he'd socked away his first million. Not that I'm any expert on employment but maybe jobs are like lovers—one day they're boring and stupid but suddenly they're real desirable when you think you're getting dumped. I don't know, he'd just broken up with his long-time squeeze when I met him, he was all set to get down and be irresponsible. Now that he's scratched that little itch deep enough for a while and he wants to act like a grown-up again he needs somebody to blame for acting like a kid. When we'd stay up late he'd sometimes get in this panic, this big middle-class guilt thing about being a productive citizen even though the night before he'd wanted to be a bohemian, right? Then he'd take it out on me, get real weird in the mornings. I mean, I didn't tell him to stay up all night, he was right there chopping the lines and pouring the drinks.

Now, after a little run with the bad girls, it's back to the mature and responsible Patty. Enough of the postmodern girls, now he wants the good old-fashioned kind. Patty's like a banker or something. I can see her in her sensible shoes with her briefcase, or her Talbot's clothes on the weekends in the country, doing the crossword puzzle, sipping decaf, buying antiques. Pass *The New Yorker,* dear. Certainly, muffin.

Dean practically has all of Shakespeare memorized and he can handle millions of dollars a day of other people's money, he can be smart about other people but he's like a foreigner to himself. Sometimes I just wanted to stand him in front of the mirror and say, Dean, meet Dean. Sit him down with himself and translate what he says into plain American.

So that's Dean. Francesca's wrong, he's not a jerk. He is, but not really. I fucked up. I did something he couldn't get over, and you can't really blame him for that.

I don't know, he did the same thing to me, screwing Cassie Hane. I suppose that was why I did it. I called up one night a few days before our killer Truth or Dare session and asked him to take me out to dinner and he said he couldn't, he had to go out with some friends. What really pissed me off is he didn't give me any explanation. That was that. You know, he could have said who these friends were who were so important and so exclusive that they couldn't stand my company, but he didn't. I said fine, really bitchy so even Dean could tell I was pissed, and hung up. Then I waited for him to call me back and the son of a bitch never did. I was furious. I was so furious I called him back after half an hour to tell him. I got his machine. After that I called up Cassie Hane's boyfriend, Peter. I didn't say who I was, I just asked if Cassie was there and he said no, she had her own place and I said, you know how she got that Barneys' ad? Dean Chasen is real good friends with the guy who owns that agency. And he goes, who is this? and then I go, a friend, I hate to see her make an idiot out of you. Then I hung up. Next I call up Cassie and I do this southern accent I can do perfectly from all the girls we used to show horses with and I go, Cassie, honey, I hate to be the bearer of bad tidings to y'all but I saw you the other night with Dean Chasen and I just thought it might interest you to know that he gave me a nasty little infection. And she goes, who is this? but I'm already gone.

So when Jeannie came home and asked if I wanted to split a gram I said sure. When that was gone we went to the

Surf Club and Didi was there, and so was Skip. Skip was flirting outrageously, really hitting hard on me, all these steamy looks and sexual innuendos. I don't know, I had a bunch of drinks, at that time of night Magilla Gorilla can start to look good and Skip's no gorilla, he's pretty decent-looking, plus I was remembering that he was actually really good in bed. Plus I was so mad at Dean. That's what it was really all about in the end, when Skip and I were rocking the old sleigh bed back at his place, we weren't really screwing each other, we were both screwing Dean.

I wish I hadn't, but it's done now. I think about calling him, but I don't. I turn on the tube for a while and watch "All My Children." Then I go back to sleep.

When I go to the doctor's I tell her I just feel shitty and nauseous and I sleep all the time. She asks me about my period and I can't really remember. I've been on the pill since I started going out with Dean but sometimes I forget to take it and I can't really remember when I finished up the package. I don't know, for a while there—like a couple of months—I was using the old withdrawal method, which is about as safe as Russian roulette. After surviving that I figure I should do fine on the pill. My gynecologist keeps telling me I should make the guys wear rubbers but I hate them and so do they. Safe sex, right? That's like, truth in advertising, it's kind of a contradiction in terms.

So anyway, I think this doctor's barking up the wrong tree, but she takes some blood for a test along with everything else and sends me on my way without a single prescription for narcotics, which really depresses me, I'm going to have to find a new doctor. I mean, when I spend a hundred bucks I usually get off.

So I meet this guy at Jackson Hole who wants to buy the necklace. The short, balding type, maybe forty, he looks like my father. He has rotten skin, the pores in his nose are like the potholes on Second Avenue, you could lose a cab in one of those things. Real attractive, right? He's wearing this incredibly tacky diamond ring and a giant Rolex. If I had to list my least favorite things, jewelry on men would be right up there at the top.

After we sit down I take the necklace out of my purse—it's in this blue velvet case—and he puts it down on the table and starts looking at me instead of the pearls. He goes, your sister Rebecca is a lovely girl, I admire her very much.

I go, she's a big hit with all the boys.

And he goes, but I think you're even prettier.

You'd be the first if you really did, I say.

Just to give him a little hint about why we're here and all, I reach over and open the case for him. He picks up the necklace and holds it up to the light, sticks a little telescope thing in his eye and squints at it. I mean, this has got to be an act, I know damn well who he's buying these for, but she certainly went to a lot of trouble to make it look authentic, the bitch.

When the waitress comes around I order a burger deluxe because I haven't eaten in two days and frankly I'm starved and I figure I'll tell him I forgot my wallet. I'm feeling really dizzy, for a minute I almost black out, my vision gets all blurry.

After a while he says, nice, not bad at all. Then he looks up and says, did you know that pearls are a symbol of purity? and I shake my head, I'm scarfing my burger.

I bet you're pure, he goes.

And I'm like, right.

And he goes, I bet you don't go out with just anybody.

So finally I've cleared this big wad of beef out of my mouth and I say to him, actually I fuck practically anybody. But in your case I think I'd make an exception.

And he's like totally blown away that I'm talking like this.

So how much for the necklace? I go and eventually he offers me twenty-five hundred and I take it, he's got the cash right there—naturally a guy who wears gold jewelry would carry a huge roll of cash, right?—so I take it and make him pay for the burger and I walk out of the restaurant feeling dizzy and puke all over the sidewalk.

And this guy who's just bought my grandmother's symbols of purity comes out and watches me wipe off my face and goes, you wanna come back to my place and lie down for a while?

I hand over most of the money to Jeannie because even though her father came up with the back rent I still owe for the past month plus the phone bill and that pretty much takes care of my little inheritance. And of course she immediately decides we should buy a quarter ounce. But I'm the irresponsible one, right? Well, okay, I am a little irresponsible and I don't protest as much as I should about this idea. But I haven't really talked to Jeannie in ages and I really want to sort of clear the air, you know, I mean Jeannie and I go way back, plus I'm feeling so bad I don't think anything could make me feel worse and it's either stimulants or another twenty hours in bed.

We just sit around the apartment and talk all night. It's great. We start talking about Didi and how great it is that she's off drugs because she really had a problem, she was just way over the top.

Next we start talking about guys, naturally. Jeannie says she doesn't know, she's just not sure about Frank, does she really want to spend the rest of her life with this guy who was kind of dull to begin with and then betrayed her with a bimbo? Frank is pushing for a fall wedding and now Jeannie's got cold feet. I tell her she knows my feelings about marriage, I mean probably it works for people with really low expectations and about zero self-esteem, but show me a happy marriage and I'll show you one fool and one hypocrite. Like, I've got a late meeting tonight, honey, don't wait up for me. Okay, darling, don't work too hard.

I don't even mention that Frank has one of the smaller dicks I've ever experienced. Two inches of throbbing steel.

So after a while we talk about the old days on the horse circuit, that was where we got to know each other, sharing rooms in half the Hiltons of America, showing and jumping while everyone else was going to school and proms, riding all year long to qualify for the three big shows in Harrisburg, Washington and then Madison Square Garden, ordering room service and flirting with the busboys and the stable hands and the judges, and now it sort of feels like all of that's ending, I mean it ended a long time ago, a few years back anyway, but in a way we sort of grew up together on the road and in the saddle and moved to New York together and now I'm moving out to Francesca's and somehow I don't think I'll see Jeannie much after a while. She really sort of screwed me over but it still depresses the shit out of me, because whatever comes next it won't be the same.

And Jeannie is all excited about something she's saying, I've been half listening, something about horses, and then she's crying, saying, that wasn't fair, that was so unfair, I still think about it.

It turns out she's all upset about this one show out on Long Island when I won the ribbon for hunters. Showing hunters is very political anyway, it's all up to the judges. With jumpers if you jump clean it's strictly against the clock and more fun. The horses are thinner and they're fast and nobody can rob you if you win. Hunters are big fat beautiful animals and they're judged on form, supposedly. And I do mean supposedly.

So this one day Jeannie went before me, she was on this horse, Patrick Henry, he was beautiful and she had a great run, everything clean, I watched her from the stand and then I went out on my horse, Eric the Red. Eric was in this really rotten mood, I don't know why, then when I get out there and start jumping I realize he's lame. He banged two jumps early on and twisted once coming down. I was trying really hard to hold him up, he was pretty lame and I just thought, go for it, let's just get through this thing.

So me and Eric the Red won first prize in the class.

Something weird was going on in that judging booth, don't ask me what. Maybe my father paid somebody, maybe somebody liked the look of my ass in riding breeches, whatever.

It was so unfair, Jeannie goes. I never forgot that.

And I go, welcome to the world, Jeannie babe.

Because that's the thing about hunters and jumpers. The jumpers are fair, it's you against a clock. But showing hunters, it's political. Great preparation for life, right?

Let's face it, how often is anything fair?

Jeannie finally stops crying long enough to tell me she's always competed with me, even though she loves me she's always tried to outdo me in everything and never felt like she could, like this is news to me, and I go, it's okay really and for about three minutes we're best friends, everything's fine, and we talk about really silly and trivial things that seem important enough at the time and finally she says, I'm going to give you the best birthday ever and then she goes whoops, like there's been a big surprise planned and she blew it.

I sort of figured my friends would do something, I mean, I hoped they would. Ten days from now I'll be twenty-one. It seems like I've been on the planet a lot longer than that. Like who is that woman who goes around the country to Ramada Inns pretending to be some forty-thousand-year-old man, charging people hundreds of dollars to come listen to her speak in this fake baritone about the wisdom of the ages? Well, whoever she is she's an imposter, the real forty-thousand-year-old man is me. And I'm here to tell you, free of charge, that it sucks.

# 12

# GOOD NIGHT LADIES

Of course with my luck it turns out I'm actually pregnant. The rabbit dies, so I have to visit the clinic for real this time. I can't believe it. And I don't have a nickel to my name, I owe everybody in the western hemisphere, I'm like a fucking Third World country—empty treasury, exploding birth rate. Jesus. And what's really depressing is I don't know whose it is, I mean, it could be Skip's and it could be Dean's. If this had happened a few months back there would've been like twenty suspects, but even two is too many. Francesca and Jeannie want me to call Dean, they say it's only fair. No way. I'd rather have the kid than call Dean, and I'm not about to have the kid.

I call Carol first, my sister, and she's really sympathetic,

I don't know what I'd do if I didn't have Carol to talk to sometimes and she says if I can't find the money anywhere else she'll get her boyfriend to cough it up, he's rich and she'll threaten him with a sex embargo if he gets difficult about it.

I go, where's Dad? and she says he's in Cancun with a new bimbo. Which is just great. Whenever I need my old man he's on some beach with a nineteen-year-old sex kitten. Story of his life.

Next I call my old man's office and his secretary claims he's in Europe on business and then she says, I just sent you the check for your school tuition.

And I'm like, incredible, I don't believe it. Something actually going right in my life for a change. I must be dreaming.

So I make an appointment for the next week and I use the tuition money which is kind of ironic because last month I used my supposed abortion money for tuition and now it's the other way around. And if that's not weird enough I see Skip Pendleton a few nights later, he's with some anorexic Click model and pretends not to see me. Meanwhile my breasts hurt like hell and I feel like I'm filling up like a water balloon. I try not to think about the thing inside me, I mean, even if it's a person instead of a fish I want to say, hey, believe me, I'm doing you a favor. You don't need this shit.

I'm so distracted that I totally forget the appointment is the day before my birthday. When I figure it out I'm like, what the fuck, I want this over with. They tell me I should be able to walk out of the clinic that afternoon and barring complications I'll be fine in a day or two. I tell them I've got twenty-four hours till the first day of the rest of my life.

* * *

Don't ask me why, I don't want anybody to think I'm getting mushy in my old age, but for some reason I decide to visit Mannie in the hospital. They've got him over at Lenox Hill, I walk over. Out in front these two old guys are having a wheelchair race down the sidewalk and people start cheering them on, these two guys must be in their eighties but they're really starting to cruise and people are jumping out of the way, then a nurse and an orderly come out and start screaming at them and chase them down.

Mannie's like a cartoon version of an accident victim, they've got him in this body cast, he's like a mummy in traction. His head is pretty well bandaged up but you can see his face and when I come in he opens his eyes, he starts smiling like a lunatic, I don't know if he remembers me or if he's just like a baby that smiles at anything.

So I go, it's Alison, Rebecca's sister. Then suddenly I feel bad, like I maybe shouldn't mention Rebecca, right?

He smiles, the guy's beaming like a headlight, either they've got him on some really great drugs or else he's glad to see me.

I'm really sorry, I go.

I know, don't tell me, I have a real gift for saying the intelligent thing.

I sit down in this chair beside the bed, just to give myself something to do. He's still smiling, it's beginning to drive me crazy, it's like he knows something I don't know, so finally I go, Rebecca asked me to send her best, she had to rush out of town for some important stuff but she wanted me to check up on you and say hello and all.

Which is totally a lie, I don't know why I say it, except maybe to make him feel better.

And after another few minutes of smiley-face I go, it was an accident, right? His face is really white, white and red where he's cut and stitched, he looks like some painting where the colors are all wrong and not true to life.

His mouth starts to move and I lean closer so I can hear what he's saying. Finally he says, in this gnarly whisper, tell her I love her.

And I'm like, what are you, nuts? You're crazy, you're really out of your mind. Listen, I go, I hate to be the one to tell you but she's actually a total bitch, she doesn't give a shit about you, she doesn't give a shit about anyone but herself, she hasn't even asked about you. That's what kind of person Rebecca is.

He's not really looking at me, he's looking through me, still smiling, and I say, what is it about her? I mean, tell me, I'm dying to know, this is really bugging me.

All he does is say it again—tell her I love her.

I say, I'm sorry, Mannie, I didn't mean that, it was just jealousy. Becca had to go out of town but she asked me to look in on you and everything. I'm sure you'll hear from her soon, I go.

I don't know if he hears me or not. I leave him grinning into outer space like some kind of Moonie, somebody way beyond your basic logic and facts. The thing is, he looks happy, which is more than you can say for the rest of us.

Francesca comes with me to the clinic. She's lost about twenty pounds in the last two weeks and she's looking great.

I make her promise not to call Dean no matter what. We sit around in this waiting room with *Mademoiselle*s and *Ladies' Home Journal*s on the coffee table in case we want to get some summer tanning tips or learn how to make a supermoist coffee cake that will drive hubby into fucking raptures and then they call me in and I undress, put on the little paper robe, climb up on the table, stick my feet in the nice cold stirrups.

I want drugs, I say, as soon as the doctor shows up.

I've heard they give you Demerol and I tell them I have this monster tolerance, forget about the correct dosage for my height and weight, but the doctor says for outpatients all they recommend is a local. I'm like, give me the express. She sticks a needle in my uterus and I try to do my sense-memory, I do a sense-memory of Dean just imagining him sitting in that chair of his where he reads and talking about Shakespeare or the stock market or something, I recreate the expressions on his face, his crooked smile, I put him right there next to me talking. Forget about sex—they're hoovering my insides out . . . the local isn't enough to kill the pain and it's hard to do my sense-memory, I can't concentrate, I keep losing the image, his face and his voice keep fading like something on a bad TV set in the middle of nowhere. . . .

So I try to remember that rhyme we used to say in school—Miss Mary Mack Mack Mack all dressed in black black black, but I draw a blank on the rest . . .

Afterwards it hurts like hell. They give me another incredibly painful shot to close up my uterus and after that it's cramp city.

Francesca takes me home in a cab and puts me in bed and Jeannie comes in with some ten-milligram Valiums and

I drift off into some kind of brain death for about sixteen hours.

Jeannie wakes me up a little after noon, she's bought me two dozen long-stemmed roses and my mail on a little breakfast tray, birthday cards from her and Carol and my mother and a bunch of other people. Nothing from my dad. Not even a fucking card.

Any messages? I go, and Jeannie says Francesca called to ask how was I doing, that's it.

So I just lie around in bed all day, I'm not exactly feeling too terrific, but why bitch?

My mom calls after five, she's very economical about little things like waiting for the rates to go down but then she'll spend a hundred and fifty dollars to have the poodle trimmed.

Happy birthday, baby, she says. You're all grown up now.

Thanks a lot, I go.

Did you get my card? she says.

I got it, thanks, I say.

Then she starts to tell me about her boyfriend, how thoughtless and inconsiderate he's been, how he's not sensitive to her needs, yada yada yada. She goes on and on, she's not blasted yet, but I can hear the ice cubes rattling at the other end of the phone. It's not like I'm not sympathetic, but it's a little depressing because maybe just this once on my birthday we could talk about me. I'm the kid here, after all, even if I'm supposed to be a big girl now. I'm the one who could maybe use some advice, and it makes me wonder, what's the point of being an adult, except that you can legally drink in all states of the union, my mom might as well be sixteen the way she talks. . . .

Finally I tell her I've got to get dressed for my party and ask if she knows where Dad is. She doesn't but she's sure he'll call.

Right.

At seven Jeannie says it's time to get dressed and helps me pick out my outfit, basic black, leather skirt from Fiorucci and a Kamali silk top, fishnet stockings, killer pumps from Bennis and Edwards that I borrowed from Didi a few months back.

You'll be raped on the street, Jeannie says after she checks me out.

I go, can't rape the willing.

That's my girl, says Jeannie.

I'm fine, I go.

Didi and Francesca have chipped in and got me a limo, so the four of us go over to Sam's and meet the gang there, a table for sixteen, the usual suspects. Rebecca's prep Everett is there, don't ask me why, he's like all mopey and it's like being at my birthday will at least remind him of Rebecca a little bit so he can keep being miserable. Plus Didi and Whitney and Mark from the tanning place and a bunch of other idiots who are all my friends sort of, and when I walk in everybody jumps up—happy birthday, Alison!—and I'm looking around thinking just maybe Dean will be there but he isn't and why would he be, really?

So we have this big dinner, I mean, some of us have this big dinner and some of us just keep going to the bathroom, Jeannie's got blow and so does Mark, Didi keeps screaming at us saying we're fucking drug addicts, she's really disgusted. It's amazing she doesn't even see that it's like pretty ironic, to say the least. When we all do a chorus of "Amazing Grace," she gets really mad.

Things kind of get out of control after a while. The prep tries to beat up the waiter, don't ask me why. He's one of those fighting drunks, plus his heart is broken. He offers to marry me at one point and I say, thanks, but I don't believe in marriage and he goes, I can respect that point of view, saying the words real carefully like he's afraid he'll drop them and they'll break. Then he offers to pay for the meal and everybody thinks this is a cool idea, suddenly he stands up and bangs on a wineglass with a spoon until he breaks it, so then he pounds on the table till he gets everybody's attention and then he looks around like he's not sure where he is until suddenly he remembers. He weaves his head like he's ducking a tiny plane that just skimmed the top of his hair. Then he goes, really serious, today is Alison's birthday.

Everybody goes wild and cheers, partly because it seems amazing that he can even talk or remember what the occasion is.

Today, he goes, Alison is an adult.

A lot of catcalls and hisses for this idea. The prep takes a direct hit—a piece of cheesecake on the cheek.

I'm serious, he goes. I mean this. I love this girl, no, wait, she's not a girl now she's a woman.

So of course Didi and Francesca start singing Bob Marley's "No Woman, No Cry."

Everett waves his arms for silence, his right hand is still bandaged from where Mannie cut him, he's like, I love her sister, but I love her too. I'd like to treat Alison and all of you to dinner because you're all friends of Rebecca's and I love Rebecca and I love all of you.

So everybody's cheering and throwing shit at the prep and I have this funny feeling about this offer. Sure enough, he remembers when the waiter brings him the check that he gave Rebecca all of his credit cards.

Later we go to Nell's and then the Zulu Lounge and then we end up at our place but it's too small and the prep says he's still got this suite over at the Stanhope, he can't afford to pay the bill so he keeps staying on. So we go over there, it's getting toward dawn by now and Jeannie takes up a collection and makes a run over to Emile's place. . . .

The party goes on for two days.

Some of the people disappear eventually, some come back the second night, two guys from this Australian rock band drop by for nine or ten hours and Emile shows up with fresh supplies, I guess we must've called him. Francesca keeps coming and going, trying to rescue me, at one point she offers to take me shopping at Bergdorf's with her Dad's credit card but me and Everett hold down the fort, sitting in the middle of the floor going, I can't believe somebody else feels that way—wow, I thought I was the only person in the world who felt like that—and him telling me about Rebecca and me talking about Dean while I burn holes in the upholstery of the Louis Cathouse chairs. We just can't talk fast enough to free up all these great thoughts we're having. Great minds sink alike, right? So at some point I ask Everett if he knows the three great lies. I tell him the first two while he sits there nodding like a guru or something with like the intense calm that only the truly crazed and manic can fake. Then I say to him, so what's the third?

That's easy, he says. The third lie is, I love you.

And I'm thinking, wow! of course. That's it!

And we have to phone in booze and cigarettes from this deli over on Lex because they've cut off our room service and I try to call my dad but I can never get him and I remember something about the management saying we would have to leave but we shined them on basically and after that I don't know, I think I got hysterical at some point, maybe I tried to jump out the window, suddenly it seemed like the thing to do.

Anyway, somewhere in the depths of my delirium tremendous I have this flash of sanity that says I am in bad trouble and I remember this thing in my wallet, so at some point when old Everett is draining his toxins I dig through my purse and then my wallet and finally come up with the card, which is tucked up behind the change purse with all these napkin fragments with the names and numbers of all the boys I never called and I crawl over to the phone and call out, call this number, the last four digits spell out H-E-L-P on the dial.

I think after that I talked to my father, I'm not sure, but anyway, eventually a doctor comes over to the suite, I don't really remember. . . .

And now I'm in a place in Minnesota under sedation dreaming the white dreams about snow falling endlessly in the North Country, making the landscape disappear, dreaming about long white rails that disappear over the horizon like railroad tracks to the stars. Like when I used to ride and was anorexic and I'd starve myself and all I would ever dream about was food. There are horses at the far end of the pasture outside my window. I watch them through the bars.

Toward the end of the endless party that landed me here I was telling the prep the story about Dangerous Dan. I had eight horses at one point, but Dangerous Dan was the best. I traveled all over the country jumping and showing and when I first saw Dan, I knew he was like no other horse. He was like a human being—so spirited and nasty he'd jump twenty feet in the air to avoid the trainer's whip, then stop dead or hang a leg up on an easy jump, just for spite. He had perfect confirmation, like a statue of a horse dreamed by Michelangelo. My father bought him for me and he cost a fortune. Back then my father bought anything for me. I was his sweet thing.

I loved that horse. No one else could get near him, he'd try to kill them, but I used to sleep in his stall, spend hours with him every day. When he was poisoned I went into shock. They kept me on tranquilizers for a week. There was an investigation—nothing came of it. The insurance company paid off in full, but I quit riding. A few months later, Dad came into my bedroom one night. I was like, uh-oh, not this again. He buried his face in my shoulder. His cheek was wet and he smelled of booze. I'm sorry about Dangerous Dan, he said. Tell me you forgive me. He muttered something about the business and then passed out on top of me and I had to go and get Mom.

After a week in the hatch they let me use the phone. I call my dad. How are you? he says.

I don't know why, it's probably bullshit, but I've been

trapped in this place with a bunch of shrink types for a week. So just for the hell of it I go, Dad, sometimes I think it would have been cheaper if you'd let me keep that horse.

He goes, I don't know what you're talking about.

I go, Dangerous Dan. You remember what you told me that night. After he died.

He goes, I didn't tell you anything.

So, okay, maybe I dreamed it. I was in bed after all, and he woke me up. Not for the first time. But just now, with these tranks they've got me on, I feel like I'm sleepwalking anyway and I can almost believe it never actually happened. Maybe I dreamed a lot of stuff. Stuff that I thought happened in my life. Stuff I thought I did. Stuff that was done to me. Wouldn't that be great? I'd love to think that ninety percent of it was just dreaming.

Jay McInerney's bestselling novels, *Bright Lights, Big City* and *Ransom,* have been published in more than a dozen languages. His recent fiction has appeared in *Esquire* and *The Atlantic,* among other magazines, and he also wrote the screenplay for the movie version of *Bright Lights, Big City.* A graduate of Williams College, he has held fellowships from Princeton and Syracuse universities. He lives in New York City.